W9-AQK-169

ANDRÉ NORTON
FORERUNNER:
THE SECOND VENTURE

A TOM DOHERTY ASSOCIATES BOOK

This is a work of fiction. All the characters and events portrayed in this book are fictional, and any resemblance to real people or incidents is purely coincidental.

FORERUNNER: THE SECOND VENTURE

Copyright © 1985 by André Norton

All rights reserved, including the right to reproduce this book or portions thereof in any form.

First printing: August 1985

A TOR Book

Published by Tom Doherty Associates
8-10 West 36 Street
New York, N.Y. 10018

Cover art by Victoria Poyser

ISBN: 0-312-93256-1

Printed in the United States of America

1

This was scraped land, laid bare to heat-roasted rock, lacking a single lift of withered leaf or stem to break the unending stretch of gray-blue stone seamed with darker cracks. Still a cloak-covered body crouched above a winding fissure, one that ran from horizon to horizon across the desert world. Only in that fissure itself was there movement, a thick, ever-forward lapping—not of liquid, but rather heaving sand, swirling slowly along.

There was no sun to beat and blast this wasteland, nothing but open sky overhead. Open until the eyes reached above far enough to mark that screen of haze lidding this simmering pot of a planet.

The cloak shifted a fraction. Within the cave made of its folds there was small movement. The soft touch of tight curled antennae, the sharp prick of a claw against pillar of arm.

"Think you I have been a fool, my Zass?" The voice was not a whisper or a murmur, rather came as a croak from dried lips, the words hard shaped by a mouth as moistureless as the land. "Ah, Zass—there is folly, and there is choice—against that which is worse."

The mound of cloak heaved as the wearer it completely covered straightened, lifted her head to peer through the opening between two folds at that sliding of what was not water yet still passed walls of naked stone.

"Folly . . ." There was a bitter tinge to that single word. Even as she admitted to so much, another emotion arose, stark as the land, clear as the rock of any trace of life. Fear had moved her, brought her into this furnace of death, a greater fear than she had known before.

Again the cloak rippled. Simsa closed fingers tightly about that possession which, living, she would never discard. It was not a staff, not long enough for that—rather more a rod of office such as headmen of river towns in the world she had known might carry on occasions of state. Even under the folds of the cloak it shone—the disc at its head, the two curved horns on guard at the sides. Sun and two moons, she had once been told.

"Thom!" Her tone made a spat oath of that name. The sound seemed to please her, for she said it once again with more force, a further unleashing of fury. "Thom!" She did not call. Could any voice reach from world to world, lift upward through sky to the emptiness of space—wing from world to ship, ship to world, and bring it to the right ears?

It was Thom who had introduced her to *them*—those cool-voiced, veiled-eyed men to whom he had shown respect, whom she had suspicioned from first meeting. She who was—

Again her shoulders shifted. Paws patted lightly against her firmly planted forearm, a small, sharp-snouted face turned up to hers. Those other thoughts, so alien and yet meant to please, to reassure, nibbled at the edge of her mind.

"I am Simsa. . . ." She said that slowly with a space of a breath before each word. Simsa—and who else?

Once she had been a light-fingered errand runner for an old and crafty woman who knew much and told little enough. With Ferwar she had sheltered, as far back as her body memory reached, in the Burrows below the city pile of Kuxortal. She had soaked up, as might a sagser root given water, all that could be learned. Still she, even in Ferwar's days of whining command over her, had been free—

Free as she could, would, never be now! There were degrees of freedom; at least she had come to learn that!

Freedom she had won from the Burrows, only because she had had her fortune twined for a space with that off-worlder who had sought his lost brother—and the secret that brother had hunted in turn. Though she had inwardly rebelled, the stubborn-held life spark within that Simsa had sent her with him into a trap of ancient death and new-come disaster.

Then . . . She lifted her rod of sun-and-moon, with a hand she had not consciously set to that task, so that the tips of the curved moons touched her small, high, near childish breasts. Her head snapped up; the flow of energy that she thought had forsaken that ancient artifact was not exhausted! Into her now flowed, not the power of destruction she had once called upon, rather a sensation of drinking deeply, feasting well. Through her coursed that reviving surge.

The girl closed her eyes to the opening between cloak folds, seeing once again the waiting one—the other Simsa, a mirror copy of herself. Or, rather, perhaps she was a reflection of that one. At a single touch she had become two, who for a space were wary, jealous of their mutual possession— the Simsa whose black skin now contained them both.

Only for a space had that been so. Then she was one again, but a new one. Scraps of knowledge, of which a Burrows child could never even dream, found space and rooted. She had been triumphant, proud, a great one in those moments. Even Thom had seen it. Yes, but in seeing it he had also been aroused to make of her—

Zass growled deep in her long thin throat, her wings, covered in ribbed skin, lifted a fraction. Zass had always been able to catch Simsa's anger—or her fear. It had been Zass who had warned her into this last venture bringing them here.

"Forerunner," Thom had called her—talking much of very ancient star-roving peoples unknown to his later kind, who had left their touch on many worlds, still puzzles to all who strove to unlock forgotten mysteries. Forerunner—booty. As much a treasure for him and his fellows as anything grubbed from the earth, shaken clear of age-settled dust. Simsa was to go back to those who searched for such booty. None had asked her consent, nor even told her clearly what was to come.

Thom had disappeared when she had been escorted to that gaunt, space-blackened man with the eyes that looked yet did not seem to actually see. He might be gazing beyond one to search for some value. In her then the Burrows Simsa had stirred awake, and even the ancient Simsa had withdrawn to consider and study and plan. . . .

Save that they had not had too much time together, that first Simsa and she from the past. The Burrows-born girl had extended claws and waited to defend herself. Though she had known she dared not call upon the destructive powers centered in that very rod she fondled now, as she relived what had happened. An animal threatened will flee or attack. Simsa—neither Simsa had ever fled. To attack—that was also wrong, the wrongness ground into her sharply. Violence was not the answer to these spacepeople. There were wilier ways. Wait, learn, the Elder One cautioned. Learn what they have to offer—whether it will be of benefit or ill. Weigh the ill—if it be the greater, then plan secretly.

So she had gone aboard the ship without protest. Three zorsals she had had, the two young males she had loosed to their freedom in the skies of their own world—her world. But Zass clung to her and would not be sent away. And, in a way, she clung to Zass as fiercely, a reassuring fragment of the life she had always known.

Simsa had never been aboard a skyship before. Much was strange there, made even stranger by the fleeting scraps of memory that had awakened in Elder One when led to compare with the far past. She surrendered to that second Simsa all save a scrap of her long-held will, evading questions of these strangers, asking others of her own. Thom might well have been within the metal skin of the ship which lifted with them, but she had not seen or heard from him.

In the small cabin they had given her for her own place, she had discovered, to her great anger, held rigidly in check, certain small hidden things by which she could be overlooked whenever these space rovers wished. The Burrows Simsa would have torn them loose, smashed them. The Elder One cautioned otherwise. Before each of those hidden spies she had used her rod. Then it was clear that anyone seeking to overlook her would see what was most in their minds concerning her. Meanwhile she was about her own business—that of escape.

The finding of the spy things had not only aroused hot Burrows anger, but impeccable purpose. These off-worlders wanted her for what they could learn. Just as they desired the place from which her twinned self found a storehouse of knowledge, though it was a tangle of ancient wrecked ships being mined by outlaws for unique weapons to be sold to the highest bidders on many different worlds.

From her these strangers sought to draw knowledge not theirs to have or hold, which she was in no mind to surrender. Simsa lay on the sleep place in that prison of hidden eyes and ears, Zass curled by her. And, closing *her* eyes, she began questing as she would never have believed could be done, but which the Elder One, pressing with her stronger will, found natural.

There was a wild whirl of thoughts pulsing throughout the ship. To plunge into that was like jumping into high sea surf where currents broke about reefs. Simsa of the Burrows struggled feebly, lost. She was drawn along as that other sought her own way of keeping track of these voyagers.

There were two who had centered their innermost attention upon her own self. Sealing away all clamor of others, Simsa followed those thought trails to what lay behind. One was a healer of sorts—a woman whose pitifully small fund of knowledge was considered large and imposing by these others. She was concerned with flesh and bone, and only a little with that which the body obeyed. Also . . . Simsa's eyes remained closed, but her lips lifted in the snarl of a Burrower's child—this one wanted fiercely to slash, to study, to even mutilate if she must, in search of something truly indefinable which was the force of life itself and which she did not even know existed.

The other, who would learn . . . Ahh. . . . The snarl relaxed. Instead her tongue tip smoothed across the lower as one preparing to savor an exotic but promising bit of food. He did have a glimmering idea of that which had been taken from Kuxortal's planet. Even now he was considering one approach and then another. One could play sly games with such as he, if there were time.

Time! The very thought of that stung her. Thom had told her openly that what she knew would be of great interest to a race allied with him, a people whose life-span was so long that they had turned long ago to the study of the rise and fall of species, keeping vast records. Yet the time before . . . ah, the time before was Simsa's alone and she was the guardian!

Only this ship's officer, who would make her prisoner, even though as yet he had not shown his intent, had no idea of taking her to those of whom Thom had spoken in awe. He would keep her, somehow train her, for himself alone. Now she laughed silently. Oh, little man, what would best shatter that plan of yours? She could do thus—or thus— Again she laughed without a sound, though Zass stirred against her and growled.

Let him play with his plans, that one. She had other business before her now. Just as she had sent forth seeking thought, so now she sought knowledge, not of what was

living within this space-traveling shell but of the shell itself.
Some things her older memory touched upon and recognized,
yet the structure was different. As might well be, for long
ages lay between the time of a ship that had once obeyed
her and this one carrying a younger race.

She cared nothing about the source of its power. In the end
all such were not too different, and never had mechanics held
any interest for her. There were other places—places that
stored knowledge, places that might offer an escape.

The right knowledge she found while skipping randomly
from mind to mind of the crew. Yes, there was an exit and
those who were trained to use it. But as yet she was not ready
to bend another will to hers and through such a temporary
captive learn— Success was again a matter of time.

Why that instinctive need for haste beat at her so, forcing
her to wider and wider exploration, Simsa could not have
said. However, the fear of her Burrower heritage melded
with other uneasiness of the Elder One and thus she did no
probing, made no attempt to bend any other mind within this
shell to do her will. Not yet.

She was vaguely conscious of an increasing warmth. Even
though her eyes were closed, Simsa sensed that the sun-and-
moons of her rod were alight. In a way both fed her strength
for this weird voyaging of thought—as well as building in her
the imperative need for action. Was it chance, or some virtue
of the rod, that led her into a thought leap to the mind of a
crewman coming off duty and making his way along one of
the narrow corridors to meet one of his fellows?

Duty—a regular duty for this one—checking. Simsa became sharply intent.

Beyond the wall where his hand now rested, she picked up

the hazy idea of a cavity, within it another ship—a much smaller one. Yes, the Elder One identified, and the Burrows Simsa understood—an escape of a kind. Let this larger ship be injured, its powers fail—then some of those it bore across the star fields would have a way of seeking safety.

Duty—let him do his duty of inspecting the readiness of that Life Boat. The girl allowed herself to issue a thought order, uncertain as to how she could control this newly discovered power of which her Burrower half was still more than half-afraid.

He placed his hands against the wall. Facing the blankness in which her blurred half vision could see no break, he applied weight. There was a parting of the corridor's skin and he went in, scraping his body in the narrow space between small ship and the wall of the lock that held it.

There was this to be checked—and that. Each Simsa listed, knowing that such information would never be lost to her now. Room for perhaps three bodies such as hers to lie in cushioned space. She followed his thoughts as he fingered a lever, a button. About them would rise the other simple controls—a foam of protective sealing to preserve the passengers against the shock of ship-launching and of its landing.

That button set the strange brain of the ship itself at work, seeking out the nearest world that would give its passengers a chance for life. This lever would assert the right pattern for an orbital descent—and a landing. There were supplies that could be used for a space of time. Those, too, the crewman checked. Simsa released her tap upon his thoughts, drew back into her own inert body.

So, this ship was not wholly a space-borne prison as she had feared. Escape in that smaller vessel could be possible.

She centered a goodly part of her mind on that, leaving only a sentry of the Burrows Simsa on duty against discovery. There was, she realized, and knew she must busy herself with that, a good reason why the Elder One who had awaited so long the coming of her twin had not become sole ruler in her. The Burrows Simsa had cunning and training which that great one had never had to develop down the years.

Once more she quested for that officer who desired her, who was tempted, who wanted power. He was not with the others but alone—and he was building thought by thought to action, examining one proposal against another. A net! Yes, a net such as a fisherman would draw. A net wherein to catch her—hold her. How? This ship he might indeed command. But she was certain that he proposed not to share with another any part of what he was planning. The Life Boat!

For a second Simsa was astounded. Then she picked up the most vivid picture as if the eyes of her body saw this thing. Herself, drugged, sleeping, and this would-be possessor of power casting off in the Life Boat, bound into space. Now his thoughts hazed, became a whirling circle of small bits of desire which might have been lifted from dreams. He strode through all of these like a conqueror in a world his own will might have laid waste.

Simsa opened her eyes, cut the questing tie. There was the slight sound of metal against metal as that hand-sized hatch through which had come food and water opened.

She reached out for the cup of liquid. It appeared pure water, but she distrusted now everything within this prison of a ship. Simsa offered it to the zorsal. Zass dipped a beak to stir the surface of what was within the cup. She did not suck, instead her head swirled a fraction on her long neck as she looked to Simsa, uttering the smallest of croaks, raising her wings a fraction.

Simsa sat up, setting the cup back on its tray. For all their greedy feeding when food and drink were before them, the zorsals possessed keen senses of both taste and smell, far keener than any humanoid Simsa had ever met.

She took up the rod and held it above the cup. Slowly a greenish tinge, so faint that it could only be seen by one who, as herself, was searching, polluted the water. No poison. No, they were too intent upon squeezing her dry of all they could learn. Was this of the man's devising or a trick of that so-called healer who would be called then to minister to the ill and so get time for some of the examinations she wished?

It did not matter. Simsa slipped off the sleeping shelf and visited each of those spy buttons. Though the effort was weakening she changed the projected images she had set up there—strove to seal new ones in place before she stood in the center of her small prison, Zass on her shoulder, her hands both closed tightly about the stem of the rod, thinking.

Had that drug been given by the man, then it was close to time when he must act. Of the two she thought him the greater threat. How soon would he be on his way *here* to see how his plan had worked? If he was the one who spied upon her, and she thought he was, he would see her drink the water, fall back upon her bed, Zass also asleep across her breast. Would that image hold long enough? When she would not be here to reinforce it?

Already she had taken two steps forward to the door. It was undoubtedly locked, though she had not tried it. Now she traced the outline of its length and breadth with the moon crescent tips.

The compartment door opened. Zass took off from her shoulder, hovered in the air beating her wings, her beaked head turning from side to side to view either end of the corridor before the curve of the passage made further sight impossible.

Simsa needed no contact with the zorsal. As all her kind, Zass had not only superior sight but also hearing. With the zorsal now on guard, the girl found the lock holding the Life Boat without any worry she would not be warned. Though, as she made her way there, she was surprised to find the passages so empty. It was almost as if they had been cleared to draw her into some type of trap. So strong was this impression that as she paused along the way, her attention ever upon Zass, she also released, in a little, her own questing sense.

Now at her goal, she opened the hatch of the small podlike escape ship—an easy exercise, perhaps made so by the very fact that those who might depend upon it for escape could come here injured or even shocked near to madness by whatever catastrophe made escape necessary.

For a long moment she merely looked within, studying those same buttons and levers that she had seen the crewman test, drawing out of memory his knowledge of what was necessary for those taking shelter in the pod.

Now . . . the larger ship. Though Simsa of the Burrows had but the most limited knowledge of a space ship, and the Elder One whose awakened self had melded with hers knew ships far more intricate than this, she had some idea of the fact that there were indeed two spaces—one that made each star (to those looking up from planets) but a pinpoint of light far removed, and that other which was far different—a kind of timeless, distantless place or nonplace into which the ship

entered for a lengthy voyage and which would be unmeasured
by man, only by the highly developed, thinking machines. So
might a ship travel between spaces Simsa of Kuxortal could
not even measure.

Now—if an escape pod was loosed while the ship was in
this no-time, no-space sea, would it indeed transfer those in it
into real time, onto a real planet, or would it and its passengers be lost forever, to float in that place without future?

Still, it had been fashioned for escape. And all the acci-
dents that could happen to the parent ship and make its use
necessary—were they only to occur in normal space, in the
orbiting of a planet, perhaps? If that were so . . . Simsa held
the rod between her palms and it gave gentle heat to where
the coldness of fear had begun to stiffen her body and send
dark fingers of foreboding into her mind.

There was a sharp hiss from behind her—Zass had entered
the lock and her message of warning was plain. Unconscious
of what she did or why, Simsa slid into the Life Boat, the
zorsal once more settling upon her, wide-held wings over her
breasts.

Her entrance—what had she done!

Fear arose in a wave of harsh terror which once again
overflowed the ancient Simsa, leaving only the girl of the
Burrows cowering against the padded resting place. Whether
or not the Life Boat was meant to be used now, it was
reacting to her entrance as it had not to that of the spaceman—

It was as if she had been felled by a blow struck by one of
the slinking lawless males of the Burrows. Into dark Simsa
whirled, both her selves cut off from light, thought, perhaps
even life.

She awoke almost with the same speed as she had been

struck down. How long had she lain there? Time had no meaning. But her thoughts stirred along with her body. There was no mistaking the vibration of this small craft which held her as tightly as a shell enclosed the shapeless form of ant-crab. The Life Boat was clearly set on its own voyage—into the place where space was not—or bound for the nearest planet, to a point where her recklessness had launched it.

There was nothing she could do but wait—and neither Simsa of the Burrows nor the ancient one she was twin to could lie easy under that curtain of the unknown. Zass hissed but she did not move, except to raise her head a fraction so that her large beads of eyes met directly those of the girl. There was no fear in them, and Simsa knew a spark of pain and guilt. To the zorsal she was the protector, the all-powerful, and the creature was content to await the girl's action.

There was nourishment in containers within reach of Simsa's hands as she lay. These held no threat of drugs, so she shared with the zorsal a bulb to be squeezed so that a slightly sourish tasting water refreshed them, and she divided, amid falling crumbs, a cake of compressed dry rations.

Time did pass under a fashion. She slept, and perhaps Zass did, too. There was no break in the vibration of the humming walls. Purposely Simsa tried to wipe from her mind all but a single fact. The craft that bore her had been fashioned to preserve life. All the efforts of those who had formed it had been bent only to that one cause. Therefore let her believe that she would emerge unharmed.

Three times the feeding procedure came and went, and then there was a difference in the feel of the craft. Simsa was tempted to send out thought, but that needed another mind to link—and here there was none save herself and Zass.

The vibration's thrum grew louder until the girl curled into a ball, her fingers thrust into her ears to deaden a sound that was as painful as any cut of a Guild Man's lash back in the stews from which the Burrowers came.

Pain from that rousing whine—then a crash. Simsa's body was driven back against the far wall of the craft by the force of that. Her head cracked against uncushioned metal above the bed place. But, through the agony of that blow, she saw that same door which had closed to entrap her raising in a series of jerks. Finally it stuck and, on her knees, Simsa now brought up both hands to push, for a moment forgetting the rod. Zass squeezed through the opened slit and a moment later Simsa heard the zorsal give tongue in sheer fury and pain.

That brought her to her senses and she swung the rod upward, centering all her will on winning free. The door shuddered, began to glow. Heat from it fanned back against her own nearly bare body. Still she held until, with a last clang of protest, whatever had jammed it gave away and she was able to pull herself up and out—upon the refuge world.

That had been three days past. Simsa stirred within the cloak she had made from two stored coverings in the Life Boat. No moon, no sun—the haze would darken and so suggest night for a time, then flame again into this baking fury. The boat had landed close to this flowing stream of sand. Having no other guide, she had started to walk along that, well aware that the downed craft would be broadcasting an alarm steadily. She had no mind to meet any would-be rescuers until she knew who—or what—such would be.

They had come a long way, she carrying Zass under the shelter of her enveloping cloak, for the zorsal could not stand the heat reflected from the rock. She had traveled by night, and in the day there was nothing in the way of shelter—only this ever-stretching rock and the moving river of sand.

Though she had dug a little into the river, she had found not a hint of moisture and she had no idea what moved it with a visible current. The bag of supplies from the boat were all that now stood between them and a death that would leave dried remains of girl and zorsal on the never-changing rock.

2

Though she had slept, or rather lost consciousness in an unquiet doze, Simsa was well aware that she had near reached the end of her strength. There had been no change in the land, no sign that these plains of rock had ever supported life as she knew it. Still a feeling was also always with her, growing the stronger when she stopped to rest at the coming of greater heat, that she and Zass were not alone, that her shuffling advance was observed and weighed. She had searched the air uselessly for sight of a sharp-eyed flyer, glared back at rock until her eyes ached and teared. Nothing.

Nothing but the silent slip of the sand river. Not for the first time Simsa put Zass gently to one side and, pulling the cloak well under her to shield her bare flesh from the heated stone, lay belly flat to stare at that strange ever-flowing current. There was something about the queer eddies that now and then troubled the yellow-gray surface that kept her from investigating by touch. Also, where could she find a branch or such to prod beneath that same scum-thick surface? Her rod she would not so defile.

She had no way of telling the passing of true time here, but she was sure that the haze was darkening and that soon it would be time to move on again. If she could force herself to rise, to set her feet on the still warm rock . . . But to go where? There was nothing ahead, certainly—at least she could see nothing. She did not even turn her head to look again.

Had she been an utter fool? There was still the craft down on a shelf of this same rock, and it would afford shelter of a sort, as well as the beacon calling for help. Simsa caught her lower lip between her teeth and bit down hard. To be forced to return, to be proven a failure—neither part of her welcomed that, as sensible as such a solution would be.

Below her the sand eddied in a wider sweep. There puffed up into her face such a vile stench as set her coughing, gasping for air to clean her nostrils and lungs. Simsa raised herself on her hands but still did not withdraw from the stream side.

There was ancient rot in that puff of air. However, with it also a hint of moisture, befouled beyond belief, perhaps, but still moisture. Now she sat upright, allowed her cloak to slip away while her hands went to the single garment she wore. Since that Simsa of the deserted city had reached out to her, the Burrows Simsa, while standing alone in her gemmed crown, necklet, and bejeweled metal-strip kilt, she had taken the garb of that image from which the spark of life had come to mingle with her own. After, she had worn proudly the dress of that Elder who had ruled a people long since forgotten. Now she loosed one of the strips of the kilt, began to bend and twist it where it was made fast to the girdle until it snapped, giving her a silver metal strip studded with gems that could be cloudy or awake under certain lights to brightness. It was longer than her arm by a little. She held it firmly by the portion twisted free of the intricate linkage to plunge into the disturbance of sand which spread farther both up the river and down.

For a very long moment she hesitated. Certainly that whiff of foulness was no invitation to investigate further. But the sliding sand was all that might stand between her and an impotent trip back to the Life Boat.

Her Burrows memory was wary, yet that also could give way to impatience. And now it did. As she might have used a short stabbing spear on some of the beshelled crawlers of Kuxortal's faraway coast, so did she bring the gemmed strip down with all the force of her arm.

It entered the sand easily enough, but—

Simsa flinched. Somewhere below that curling of gray brown she had struck opposition. Something she had attacked was moving, first threshing wildly about so that its frenzied struggle caused an upheaval not unlike a minor eruption. A bubble of the thick stuff broke in the parched air, releasing concentrated odor so foul that Simsa felt instant nausea.

There was nothing else moving, not even when she tried to draw forth her improvised probe. The metal held as stiff and straight and opposed to her strength as if it had pierced whatever it had first encountered, pinning it to the rock bed.

Simsa shrugged off the last part of the covering across her shoulders and arose to her knees, hands tightly clutching the strip. No strength she could put forth moved it. She began to weave the probe back and forth. At first the obstruction was so great she could not stir her metal length no matter how hard she tried. Then it began to give. There was a sudden falling away on one side. Simsa answered that with as sharp a twist as she could deliver. Almost she lost her balance as the final release came. The strip popped up into view, scattering great sand droplets in all directions, bringing a miasma of the stomach-turning stench with it intensified to the hundredth part.

It did not come cleanly, though the sand of the stream did not cling to it. Rather there was, impaled on the tip, a thing as large as her two fists together. It was of that thick yellowish color shown by pus draining from a wound. And it moved constantly in a wild writhing, as if it strove to tear itself from the metal centered in its body.

In shape it was an ovoid, with no marked features nor any head or tail parts. From its underside spread, to lash in the air, eight tentacles, all of the same size.

Simsa knew the dark spinners of the Burrows. But those were well favored compared to this noxious blob. She held it well away from her and the rock shore, studying it as best she could. This was the first life she had seen since she had crawled out of the craft.

It was contracting those legs or limbs, wrapping them about its body as if, having found it could not escape through its original efforts, it was protecting itself as best it could.

Simsa blinked.

This nasty yellow blob was her captive. Had the constant heat, the lack of food or more than a sip or two of water, so taken over her senses that she was seeing dream projections, like those the crax chewers were said to have haunt them in the latter stage of their addiction?

It was not true! Loosing the grip of her right hand, though still balancing the improvised spear with the other, she rubbed her fingers across the heat-tormented eyes in her seared face. There was now clinging to her rod a man! Fully humanoid, clothed, and no more than two fingers high. And when the man turned his face to look to her, she knew his face—too well.

To the credit of the toughness of the Burrows Simsa, and the command of the Elder One, she neither cried out nor dropped the rod. Instead, her wrist wavering a little in spite of all her efforts at strict control, she pulled the strip back from above the sand river and tossed it to the bare rock at a point as far from her as she could send it.

Zass's hissing, which had begun when Simsa first probed into the opaque flood, arose to a scream. In spite of the heat the zorsal took to the air, flying over the girl's strange catch in the narrow circle of her species when attracted to some prey. Yet she made no move to launch herself into a swoop.

Simsa had to move the strip and shake it vigorously to detach her impossible catch. The little man lay on the rock, his chest heaving, his tiny hands pressed tight to his middle, the blood of a wound spurting a red flood over his body. His head turned so that he looked at her with such an accusing face that she dropped the strip, clasped her hands together so that her claws blood-scored her own skin. This was not the truth! both Simsas clamored in her mind. She had not brought out of that sandy river this living miniature of Thom!

Still the thing looked upon her as Thom might have appealed for her help, and she remembered all their wanderings

and those days in the city of ruined ships, days in which, in a
way she still did not understand, he had come to mean more
to her than any one she had ever known—closer in a new
way than even Ferwar, who had protected her since childhood.

"You are *not!*" She was not aware that she spoke aloud
until she heard her own voice. Zass had fallen silent, though
she still circled in the air about the wounded thing which was
not, Simsa insisted, real.

The Elder One within her now struggled for command.
This once, Simsa of the Burrows did not instinctively brace
herself in defense. Perhaps things as strange as this were
common off world, perhaps it was—

"It hides!" Again she spoke out loud, only now in the
singsong that was the Elder One's own tongue. "It bends the
sight, taking from the mind some favorite image to hide
behind. But it is a foolish thing, else it would know the
difference—"

So far had the reasonable explanation of the Elder One
proceeded when the shock of new happening hit the Burrower
girl. Even she could not believe in a manikin as big as her
flattened hand. But—that was gone! Here was a full-sized
man no different from the Thom she had known, save that he
writhed on the rock where his blood pooled. And there was
the glaze of coming death in his dark eyes.

"Small to large!" chattered Simsa, her body ashake. "I
know," she told herself, told the Elder One, "that this is not
true! *No!*"

She grabbed at the strip of metal and used it fiercely to
prod the dying man-thing—rolling it backward toward the
river. It did roll—which, she told her dazed mind, no true
man of proper size would do! So rolling, it was edged by a

last push out over the sand flow, to strike the solid-appearing surface and be sucked under. While Simsa, breathing in deep gasps of the burning air, stared downward.

Illusion; both her memories, united, held to that stubbornly. Nothing but illusion. But what kind of thing could reach into *her* mind without her being aware and pick out such a memory, use it to protect itself? Was it in truth even that blob of yellow which she had first drawn forth? Or was its true body pattern something else again? Had it worked upon her with intelligence or by instinct? She thought of how she had kept so close to the sand river in all her travel across this barren world and felt more than a little sick. Her imagination was only too ready to paint for her what might happen to someone who lay asleep, who had no barriers. Suppose the projected Thom had come across her in the early morning when she had made her rough camp here? Supposing he could have spun some tale of following her— Yes, she would have been wary of him, of any spaceman now—but was wariness such as that enough?

Zass alighted on the rock not far from the puddle of blood left behind by the river-thing. It had been swift-flowing crimson when it had worn the seeming of Thom. Now it was a dirty yellow, looking like rancid grease that had gone uncleaned from a pot far too long.

The zorsal extended her neck. Her feathered antennae pointed to the slight depression in the rock where that fluid had been cupped. Her pointed snout quivered. Then she gave a half leap into the air, instantly stabilized by wing spread— and her hissing was sharp, so that she even seemed to spit in the direction of the congealing stain.

Simsa pulled up to her feet, drawing the cloak in folds

over her shoulders. The place where the captured thing had rolled, to be once more hidden in the river, had not smoothed. There the surface of the sand flow was troubled as a larger excrescence rose above the general level.

Bigger—larger— Sand sloughed away from it. A thatch of closely cut dark hair first, and then a face with those curiously tilted eyes that had been the first strangeness she had marked in her initial sighting of Thom. The head arose until the sand formed a frill about the throat. The mouth opened, something that might even be akin to a voice topped the swish of the flowing sand:

"Simsssa." A hiss near in pitch to Zass's one of anger, a slurred attempt at her name.

The girl dropped her hold on the cloak so it fell to the rock, and the heat generated by the haze above lapped the black skin on her back and shoulders. She forced herself a single step closer to that thing in the turgid flood. Between her hands, both tightly grasping it, the rod of Elder One's near unknown, untested power pointed directly at the forehead of that illusion.

"Not!" She still had control of her voice. "You are not Thom—you are not!"

As she began to concentrate her will upon action, she half expected that the fire which the rod, the tips of the moon, the mirror of the sun, projected would come to her call and blast the sand creature into nothingness. Only there was no warming of the metal cradled so between her palms—no flash of energy. Once more the mouth of the head worked.

"Simssssa . . ."

Her name—it could somehow have picked that out of her own mind. She held no wonder too unreal after what she had seen since she and the Elder One had fused, or not quite fused, into one. But she had not thought of Thom, not that she could remember, since she had begun this journey across the endless furnace of the plain. If it drew upon her memories, old or new, why not Ferwar, or half a ten-ten of others she had known all her life, and known better than the spaceman with whom she had traveled so short a number of days?

The head—it blurred, as if her questions had somehow weakened the control of that which had set it—perhaps for bait. Still a man's head, but the black hair had blanched to pure silver to match the long strains now sticky with sweat that lay on her own shoulders, sprang wiry and alive from her scalp. White brows, which lashed about dark eyes—the skin as dark as a starless sky.

"Zzzzaaaaa . . ." that dark thing called.

"No!" Not the Burrows girl who answered this time, but the Elder One. Simsa held a fan of fleeting memories which reached from her to that bodiless head, strove to weave swiftly as a chain between them. The girl whom Thom had known drew aside, the Elder One was there, and in her a new emotion stirred until she ruthlessly locked it tightly away.

"No!" She made no lengthy speech as the Elder One filled her. Instead her hands moved independently of her conscious will, weaving back and forth so that the moon tips of her power rod might be scrawling some unseen pattern on the air between them. From her throat arose a low hum broken in rhythm now and then, as if she did voice words she made no attempt to speak aloud.

That black-and-silver head wove back and forth also, straining upward until there appeared the outline of a shoulder breaking from the shifting sands—black shoulder bare of any covering. Though the head kept its eyes fixed upon her, the mouth no longer moved. Yet its writhing against the hold of the sand, the arising and slipping back of shoulders, gave credence to a struggle, as mighty a struggle as Simsa had ever witnessed.

"Aaaah—Zaaazzza!" Thrown back, the head opened wide jaws to give utterance to a scream like that of a hunting zorsal. Its eyes were now pointed heavenward. It might have been demanding aid from some presence unseen to those from off world. If it did so, it was not favored by the answer which it sought. For it was sinking back. The shoulders had already disappeared, now sand lapped up over the chin, sought the open cavity of the mouth.

The head was gone. A head was gone. Simsa would have flung up her arm to hide that hideous change from sight had it not been that she could not unhinge her fingers from their tight grip upon the shaft of the rod.

No head now, but a stretch of obscene, greasy yellow skin that was wrinkled about a single great eye. While the whole surface of the river tossed gobbets of sand into the air, spattering over the rock. A thing or a multitude of things was rising to the surface. Simsa of the Burrows would have fled. The Simsa of the Elder Ones only stepped back so that the spattering sand could not reach her. She watched the thing narrowly while the younger, lesser Simsa shared memories again—strange and horrible—of monsters and creatures so far from normal life that even to hold them fleetingly in mind made her shrink from a wash of foulness.

Still the rod wove and the Elder Simsa hummed or changed. Yet she was also on the move. Transferring her hold from two hands to one, yet keeping the horn points of the rod ever turned toward the wallowing half-seen monster that dragged itself out of hiding so slowly, the girl took up her cloak and the provision bag and the flask of water now near consumed.

Zass gave two screams, flying to the erupting sand and turning back again swiftly to circle above the girl's head.

Thus together they edged back and away from the stream that had been their guide across this stone waste. That which sought them had won free of the sand, which cascaded back into the bed as might water running from thick hide. The creature was ovoid in form, like that thing which Simsa had snared first on the strip from her kilt. Still it did not appear quite sure of its form. For there was a haziness about its outlines and within that veiling there were changes, some lightning quick and only temporary, some more lasting. Of the weaving tentacles it sprouted, four firmed, stiffened to give it legs.

Face there was none, though a portion of it upraised to suggest a very ill shaped head, that broken by a single unblinking eye. As it crouched on the same portion of riverbank where Simsa had made her camp, it shot forward ropy limbs or arms on which there were dark stains as might be given off by something rotting while still it lived. And from it, though there was no wind to send out any odor, there emerged a gagging stench.

As Simsa continued to retreat at an angle, one that would take her from the stream and yet not too far into the rock that she could lose her single guide—the sand dweller tottered up, to stand as erect as was possible on those stiffened feet. It ceased to wave its tentacles in the air, perhaps to concentrate all its strength on what it wished the most to do—take up the chase on land.

Zass screamed full-throated on a louder note than she had yet used, swung away from circling above Simsa's head toward the girl's right—the wider plain of the stone. Its surface was broken here and there by smaller fissures which did not offer any passage Simsa was aware of to a sand river. However, because they had no surface connection with one another did not mean they were not ponds or lakelets.

As might a fountain suddenly released flash the first burden of water in its pipes into the air, so above the lip of a near fissure flared an eruption of sand. Breaking through Simsa's hum came a dull thud of noise, one beat sliding into another as if the underside of the plain over which she was retreating was the surface of a drum answering to the blows of a threatening fist.

Back, she increased the speed of her withdrawal, taking the same way that had brought her here. The heavy light and heat of the haze was diminishing—though even when it reached its lowest point it still provided enough light to guide one's way.

Though she continued to keep the rod between her and that noxious yellow monstrosity, it clumped along, wavering from side to side its swollen, filthy body, leaving behind a trail of slick slime. Simsa glanced hurriedly now and then at that other fissure which still fountained, sand sweeping up over its edge to drift outward. The same partial haze that had half hidden her first possible enemy was gathering on the lip of that broken way, and she thought it well to guess that it heralded the coming of a creature similar to that which already stalked her.

The zorsal did not swoop any lower, hanging with fast-beating wings for a long moment over the fissure, screaming

with rage and, the Simsa of the Burrows realized, fear.
There was very little a zorsal feared—being one of the most
fierce and practical hunters on its own world. It could even
be flown at a man—or a woman—and swoop to tear at eyes
and cheeks. Had she not seen Zass's two sons deal death to a
serpent-thing a hundred times their size when she and Thom
had been trapped in another unknown wilderness? The zorsals
had torn out the throat of a monster no man would have
faced, even with the sharpest and keenest weapons known.

Yet Zass here made none of those punishing dives. Though
she was ready enough to point out the danger to come, she
showed no inclination to fight.

As another thought thrust in with a stroke of pure fear, the
girl dared to glance over her shoulder. Were there any more
of those fissures close to the path of withdrawal? One—she
would need to swing near to the river to avoid that. Her eyes
snapped once again to the stalker and then to the second
fissure that had shown signs of life. Yes! A long yellowish
tentacle waved into the air there, blindly, as if it sought for
some hold aloft rather than swinging down to the rock edge.

The Burrows Simsa might have run until her lungs choked
on the heated air—the Elder One held steady, in spite of the
rising struggle within the one slender black body. If the Elder
One could handle this sand-slime, then let her do it—now!
Burrow-bred Simsa could see that all that chanting and use of
the rod made no difference to this thing. Perhaps a power
designed to work on one world was useless on another.
Could she tear loose another of the metal strips that made up
her kilt—use that as a House Guard used a sword or spear?
No, the length of the free limbs that had not adopted the guise
of legs could outreach any such attempt she would make.

Out of the deepening shade of the sky haze there came a new factor into her forced retreat. The sharp crack of sound was unlike anything she had heard before—and the vibration appeared to linger on, actually echoing twice. Did the rock under her feet answer to it? She could not be sure. Perhaps the sudden movement was a shudder of her own body.

However, the effect on the yellow stream creature and that other one climbing out to join it was much stronger. Though that which walked had no mouth, yet from somewhere out of its body it uttered an answering sound—a thin wail—so high-pitched the girl hardly caught it. Its globe body began to twitch, swaying back and forth on its pillar legs. One of those legs thinned, flipped outward, becoming once again a tentacle, so that the thing was thrown off-balance and, still fighting hard to keep erect, crashed to the rock.

There was a dull plop. The ovoid body burst like a container of foulness that had held its burden far too long. Before her eyes the sand dweller began to dissolve. Twice it reared up, strove to draw about it those rags of mist that brought it the power to change, to solidify and be a living force. And each time it did, the rod in Simsa's hands quivered also—faint, very muted, it produced the same note as there had been in that shock from overhead. Perhaps it had been at last attuned to service and was no longer so impotent.

That which had striven to climb from the other fissure showed no more tentacles, and the sand thrown forth by its floundering was fast draining back into the cavity. Just so the substance of the one before her was lapping out as liquid now, a wave to flow along the slime trail its stumped feet had left. Back that noisome stuff flowed to the edge of the river. The horn points of the rod continued to sound forth their faint keening, so that Simsa now marched forward, as she had before retreated, her rod pointing to the mess on the rock, driving it back into its own sphere with the fervent hope within her that it would not, could not, summon any power again.

3

Simsa swayed in turn as the zorsal flew straight for her, coming to perch upon her shoulder, its sudden weight threatening her balance. Zass's beak-muzzle slipped along the girl's cheek in one of the creature's seldom offered caresses. Did Zass judge the trouble over? Simsa gave the sky haze a single quick glance. She needed full attention for the fissures, to pick a way that did not encroach either upon one of those or go too near the riverbank.

Now that the enemy apparently had withdrawn for a space, she could think more clearly. That sound from the air . . . It seemed faintly familiar, as if she must recognize it. Some flying thing of prey? No, never had she chanced on any life as strange as the blob creatures. If they had some equivalent in the air overhead, then she would indeed have to watch with fear.

The cries of a zorsal—there were a whole range of those,

from the sighting of prey to that squawk of triumph when the victim was safe in its paw talons. On Kuxortal there existed fumga which sought its food along the seas' edge, an eater of carrion—and the quef, said to dwell in the high mountains—of which she had been told, but which she had never seen. Now she turned her head a fraction and dared withdraw a portion of her concentration from her route, reaching for the small entrance into Zass's mind which the Elder One had shown could be used to cement yet closer the winged hunter and the girl.

"What . . . ?" She did not truly think a word, rather she fashioned as best she could a need to know.

There was the usual misty image she could expect from the zorsal, barely recognizable, since Zass's power of sight was so different. But even as she caught that lopsided vision, Simsa also guessed at what she had heard. That sound had heralded the approach of a spaceship closing orbit upon this world. That distress signal which she had not been able to quiet had already pulled in a rescuer.

Simsa hugged her arms about herself, the warmth of the rod against her breasts. Someone from the ship she had been on? That might well be—if they had discovered her gone and had checked upon the Life Boat. If so, should off-worlders low flying sweep to seek her out, how long could she hide?

Certainly to descend into any of those fissures would be the height of folly. She wondered if she dared lie flat upon the heated rock, the cloak pulled over her to conceal. But she could not remain so for long.

Simsa frowned, remembering Thom's talk of persona units, meant to center upon the body heat of another, devices as quick on the trail and far more tireless than any zorsal.

Certainly if they sought her, they must come equipped with every such device they knew.

She was also sure that there was one aboard that ship who would never let her go free if he could help—that ship's master who had seen her as a tool or weapon to move him into an area of power he had never hoped to reach. Yes, let him be in command of the search party and there would be very little chance of deceiving them by any ordinary means.

If the orbiting ship had not come from the freighter on which she had voyaged, then it would still be very sure that a search was made. They would discover the Life Boat empty, the supplies gone—therefore they would come looking.

If this had been a world such as she knew, with ground cover and even heights, she could have played a good game. She could have arranged a scene of accident that would have deceived— No one. Simsa of the Burrows spat. She knew so much, and still there were holes in that knowledge. What might have been possible untold planet-years ago could not be tried here. The discoveries of one race or species had to be refined upon by another, improvements made that could even be unknown from one ship to the next. She had listened, she had thought, she had studied all she could. No, she must believe that sooner or later those who descended from the hazed sky of this unknown planet would be able to find her.

Accepting that as not only possible but extremely probable, Simsa had to work out her answer. That depended largely upon who those would-be rescuers were. If from the ship she knew, she would face stricter captivity. But if from another— sworn as they were to the space law of assisting any survival beacon—perhaps she could work out a story. Simsa of the

Burrows took command. She had lived most of her life by cunning scheming; now let her loose her imagination.

The haze had been fast darkening. It was no more than that which might have hung above Kuxortal on an evening fast sliding into night. Her eyes slitting a little, she discovered that she was more at ease than in the glare of daylight. She gathered up her cloak and pulled it about her. Though she had gloried in the kilt and diadem, the dress of the Elder One was foreign to space travelers and she must conceal it as best she could.

She was faced with two choices—travel on into this unending rock desert with its threat of what might rise from any of the fissures, or return upstream to the boat. She could play a distraught and frightened survivor in the latter case.

In this now silent world Simsa stared down at the rod. Zass had refused to quit her shoulder after she had recloaked. She did not try to read the zorsal's mind pattern again. It was plain enough that Zass sought protection where she had always sought safety before—close to the girl.

Simsa turned to go forward once more, heading into the unknown, careful only to keep far from any break in the rock. Her pace quickened to a trot as she still busied herself with thoughts of what she must or could do when the final test came and she had to face those intent upon her "rescue."

It was certainly plain that she could not remain on this barren world indefinitely, although the Life Boat, having once found a landing, would not rise on its own, being programmed only to carry passengers to worlds with breathable atmosphere where there would be a chance of life. In no way, Simsa thought, was it fitted to judge a strange planet for any other quality.

She was still considering what part she must act if and when, listening for any airborne sound to betray a flitter questing after her, when she first noted that the haze, which not only cloaked the sky but also hid any sharp line of horizon on all sides, was decidedly darker in one spot ahead. This was the first change from the monotony of the plain she had yet sighted.

The stream she used at a careful distance as her guide angled slightly east. That dark spot lay to the west and was constantly thickening. Simsa began to trot. Heights curtained by mist? Then she might find a safe haven among those.

Shorter fissures pocked the plain closer to each other westward. Twice she made a sidewise leap and ran a few steps when an exhalation (or so it sounded) of foul air tainted the night. Still she heard no threatening lap of sand.

Simsa could soon see more clearly that which rose from the plain. A series of blocks—huge, but so squared in shape that she could not believe that they were natural formations. About the foot of three such plateaus of different sizes facing her directly the plain was darker—the dark of a fissure or another river of sand—too deep to be gauged from where she now trotted along. If that barrier followed the roots of those cliffs, she might have no way of reaching the heights at all.

The worst was true. She came out on the rim of a gully. Below swirled more of the moving sand, passing in its slow push, north to south, even as did the river she had quitted. Simsa swung south, eyeing those towering banks beyond. Though the rock rises had looked so even-surfaced from a distance, Simsa could now see that there were fissures of differing depth and length in their faces.

Only—those fissures were far too even! Nature might have

begun the work of pocking those rocks, but some purpose not so slow nor unsystematic had then taken a hand. She might have been looking at sets of windows—perhaps even entrances, if there were ladders within to be shoved into place, or if the inhabitants possessed wings.

A hiss sounded below her chin, then the prick of claws followed as Zass changed her hold, suggesting one way of discovering whether they had chanced upon a rookery of another threatening form of wildlife. Though the zorsal strove to cling to the underside of the improvised cloak, Simsa dragged her forth enough so that the snouted head with its large eyes did face those patterned cliffs. The feathery antennae which had been so tightly curled to the small skull snapped open and out—stiff and straight, pointing to those stone rises.

Zass made no sound at all, and Simsa waited. Usually there was a whine, a hiss, or even a short growl from the zorsal. Instead the girl felt the furred body against hers quiver. The head turned slowly, keeping the antennae always pointing to the cliffs. Simsa tried mind touch.

The only emotion she could pick up was a blurred picture—a suggestion rather—of bafflement that was fast becoming curiosity. Zass raised a front paw to push aside the edge of the cloak, emerging completely out of cover, though clinging still to the coarse covering with all four paws.

Those antennae began to wave, combing the air, a sign Simsa knew of old. Zass was arousing to hunt, showing no fear at all now, rather more and more interest. Before Simsa could catch and control her, the zorsal took off into the dusk, climbing steadily through the air, then swung out across that other sand river, heading for a square of deeper shadow on the nearest of the cube cliffs.

Simsa whistled that sound which had always brought the zorsal from hiding. Zass did not reappear. She had gone into the door, window—whatever that opening might really be— not to show herself again. Nor could the girl even discover that in-and-out wave of thought pattern which marked her companion. There was only silence—the dusk, and that gaping opening, a mouth that had swallowed but had not closed.

That she could leave the zorsal never crossed Simsa's mind—the Burrows Simsa who had considered the night hunter her only close touch with real emotion was now in command. She set her jaw stubbornly, advanced to the very edge of the gulf, her wary attention divided between the surface of the flowing sand and that window-door-hole into which Zass had vanished. There was no picking up the zorsal by mind touch, even when she struggled to the extent of the talent the Elder One had opened in her. Nothing! Still Simsa was somehow sure that if Zass had gone to her death in that reckless flight, she herself would have known it.

Since the zorsal could not or would not answer, then the girl must find her own path. Slowly from right to left and back again she surveyed the sand stream. There was just one place where the rock walls confining it appeared to approach each other, and that was still farther south.

She counted aloud the openings on the one level, to set deeply into her mind the one Zass had entered. Then she strode determinedly for that narrowing of the stream.

Simsa was agile, her body fine-trained to many feats of strength that would have astounded anyone not used to the dangers of the Burrows and the skills one developed there merely to stay alive, but there seemed no hope of crossing this stream. On the far side of the narrowing there did rise the wall of one of the cube mounds, but there was a space between its roots and the edge of the river broad enough for a path.

In fact—Simsa's dark tongue tip emerged and swept over her lower lip as she considered narrowly the whole position-ing of the rock ledges here. That shelf over the stream was cut in so far so that even a portion of the wall overhung it. Yes. She could mind-picture a temporary bridge here, one that could be easily drawn should any danger come from the rock plain.

If a bridge had been there, it was long gone. She dropped to sit cross-legged, trying now in her need to do what she had been wary of doing much since she had met and melded with that other Simsa. Her own only answer was a running jump to span the flood, and that she did not dare, even used as she was to falls and climbs in the lower depths of Kuxortal. So . . . what did the Elder One have to suggest?

Simsa strove to render her mind blank as far as her Burrow past was concerned. She and Thom had both made climbs aplenty in the ruined city where the Elder One had waited in her great hall for so long. But there had also been vines and ropes and all else that intelligence could call into use as aides. Here there was only rock, with not even a stunted bush or tree above, and sand which could hide—

Simsa shook her head vigorously. She was not going to remember that—not in any detail. What *had* the Elder One to offer? She squeezed her familiar self well back, called openly for the other to think or to plan, if there was any plan possible.

And—

The answer was not quite an illusion, for it would be of this world, solid, supportive as long as it was held so by concentration. Concentration—her silver-white brows twisted into a frown and her shoulders straightened. She got to her feet, still holding the moon-sun rod in one hand, its symbol rising without her willing until the moon tips touched her own forehead above her eyes.

Warmth—

Without breaking that touch or changing the line of her set stare, Simsa reached to hook fingers in the cloak which had slipped down her body. With it in her left hand, trailing across the rock, she took steps that brought her to the very edge of the river's gully.

Her left arm whirled and the cloak arose with the gesture, stiff and heavy, dragging at her fingers. She willed with all her might—and threw—

The stiff, dark fabric went out, flapping edges like a creature of real life. It settled. One of its edges touched her feet, the other, bridging the sand flow, lay well into the niche on the other side.

"Believe!" She might not have shouted that order aloud, but it was so much a part of her that it filled her whole head. There was no longer any cloak—there was a bridge, firm and steady for her feet. This was the truth! The truth!

Holding the rod steady though its points were still warming— near searing hot now—against her skin, not looking down, for even to do that was to deny the needed belief a fraction, Simsa took one step and then again. She was treading on the cloak—no, not a cloak, a *bridge*, one summoned and held by will—her *will!*

There was a bridge prepared, and she walked it. From the roots of her silver-white hair fell drops of moisture which ran down her face like tears, to drip from her chin to her breast and shoulders. The hair itself rose from her scalp in streamers that fluttered as might a lord's tower standard on a brisk and windy day.

The pain of the rod's touch was sharp. Simsa held fast. Within her there was an outgoing, a draining—still she went forward on the bridge-that-was-not-a-cloak. She stumbled, falling forward, her free hand clawing outward ahead to catch on rock. She made a last great effort and half threw, half twisted her body to follow that hold—to lie suddenly cold and very weak on rock while the warmth of the rod vanished as from a lamp that had been snuffed.

Panting with shallow breaths that seemed never to fill her lungs as she needed, Simsa shifted her body away from the edge of the drop. The ledge, which might have been cut to support a long vanished bridge, was narrow, so already she was back from its lip, bunching the now limp cloak under her as she wriggled along on her back. At that moment she could not have again lifted a hand, neither to pick up the rod now lying sullenly cold across her breast nor to reach out for some sustaining hold.

This weakness she had felt before when she had opened wide to that one who could indeed use the rod, but never to the extent that she felt it now. She could not even raise her head, though she managed to turn it with great effort.

It was true. That was where she had been—over there! And here she was. The cloak was just a roll of cloth—yet—

Her eyelids seemed too heavy to keep up, and slow, soft waves of drowsiness swept over her. No—she must not sleep, not just yet. It was as if that other part of her delivered more than safe passage and a warning. She did not know enough—she had no training in this power which drained so. She was again Simsa of the Burrows, and as that she dared not call on the Elder One, that other.

Thirst cut through her weakness first. Her mouth felt as if it were filled with sand from below. There were her rations from the Life Boat—but water she had scanted on at every meal in this bone-bare waste. It was too bad that she could not command another illusion, one that would take on life once it was summoned—a stream of clear, pure—

Simsa's head jerked and the rock on which it rested bruised her painfully. She saw—she heard—she—smelt! Not water, that was the least of her worries at the moment. No, it was what appeared out of nowhere, leaning perilously forward from a window hold above her, its head downturned so that large faceted eyes met hers.

Feathered antennae curved forward. But this was not Zass. The great creature of the rock shared no other feature with the zorsal. Most of the face or forepart of the head was those two eyes, golden in color and broken up into many, many small circles, lidless as far as she could see and opaque when she strove to reach behind them.

Where a mouth and chin should be were small black mandibles or several pairs of jaws clicking together with the sharp sound that had first drawn her attention to the indweller. There were jointed forearms clutching with double claws the sides of its hole. What she could see of the body appeared to be covered with a thick plush of short green fur. The arms—or upper limbs—were black, the skin hard and shiny, a row of spikes running from the claws up to what would be a humanoid's shoulder.

Simsa at that moment could not have pulled herself up to any defense, and she glanced from the claws of the fore-limbs, those busy clicking, to the moving mouth with an uneasiness that began to be real fear.

Anyone who had ever visited a spaceport, or heard the tales of the space rovers, knew that intelligence and "Human" classification came in many sizes, shapes, and colors. Her own striking appearance was unlike any of the other Burrow dwellers and, Thom had once told her, totally unlike any that he had seen while he was a forescout and explorer for the Zacathan record keepers, despite the fact that they had untold species and subspecies indexed in their massive historical records.

That this thing so intently observing her now was not an "animal" or a "creature" on the same level as that she had fished from the sand river was something that seeped slowly into her mind. She gathered some of her depleted force to attempt such mind contact as she had with Zass, deciding that any intelligence possessed by this inhabitant of the rock pile might be very different, if no less keen than her own.

Her attempt was a failure. She could not even raise those in-and-out hazy "picture impressions" that were her communication in depth with Zass. For the moment, apparently, the thing was just willing to stand watching her (if standing was its posture), perhaps as baffled by her as she was by it.

Then, astounded enough to let out a gasp, she was sent rolling to the wall abutting on the ledge. The wrinkled rolls of her cloak had been jerked abruptly from her, though she could see no hand or mouth to grasp it. Since one end dangled well over the drop, she could only think at first that one of the yellow bulbous creatures had hooked it from below and was preparing to climb up to where she lay.

Only the dangling end flopped up, striking half across her body as it fell as the result of another unseen pull. There was something in this action that chilled her enough to leave her cowering against the wall, watching the square of cloth instead of the creature above her. Before she could grasp at it, or make herself put forth a hand to do so, the cloak rose, straightened out flat in the air as if it were one of those flyers Thom had shown her in action—a manmade thing ready for flight.

Then it flipped over, to display its other side, before whatever power moved it so was withdrawn and the whole of it fell back. She had just time and wit enough left to grab it before its folds vanished down toward the swallowing sand. Once more she was free to look up at the stranger above.

Sitting on one plush-covered shoulder was Zass!

The zorsal looked as thoroughly at home as if Simsa herself offered it a perch. But its antennae were completely uncoiled and the one nearest to the massive-eyed head touched a similar appendage on the alien, its tip curled a fraction about the much larger and more feathered sense organ of the stranger.

Swiftly Simsa attempted contact with the zorsal. And was again astounded. Only once before had she ever met such a wave of joy and sheer ecstasy. Once when, with her rod, she had managed to heal a broken wing that had so long kept Zass from the air and the flight the creature considered its proper sphere. Yet Zass had not been healed of any hurt this time. There was no reason for such waves of joyful emotion.

It was Zass herself who arose at last from the perch on the alien's shoulder, and the inhabitant of the rock made no sign or move to prevent the flight, remaining motionless, its wide and lidless eyes fixed on Simsa. That it had some agency to lift the cloak she was sure, though for what purpose she had no notion—unless to impress her with the fact that it had powers she might find difficult to face.

Zass landed on her shoulder, pushing a furred body close to her head, nuzzling her cheek with sharp muzzle, Zass's bid for full attention and cherishing.

Absently Simsa answered as she always had, putting up her left hand to scratch between the roots of the zorsal's antennae.

"Power—much power—"

No, that comment had not come from Zass, though in a way it had filtered through the zorsal's limited mind. Simsa was sure of the origin of the words which had seemed to boom directly into her ears, though all she still really heard was the clicking of a set of mandibles.

"Who are you?" she asked aloud, because that still came the easiest, but at the same time she thought—tried to think—to Zass as if the zorsal were one of those communication devices she had seen in use by Thom and the other spacepeople.

"Come!" The big head leaned farther out of the rocky opening, loosing both appendages from their claw grip on the stone, stretching down toward her.

Simsa wavered to her feet. Her body still felt as if she had suffered a perilous illness. This ledge led no place, and it would seem she really had no choice now. That she could once more make the inanimate obey her command, fashion a bridge, she doubted completely. The Elder One had withdrawn to her own place for now, only Simsa of the Burrows was here.

She looked at those claws which moved slightly, thinking of them curved about her wrists, choosing to tighten—to cut— Yet that instinct of awareness of danger which had been her shield so often in the depths under Kuxortal did not come to life now.

Simsa somehow knotted the cloak to hold about her waist, then planted herself facing the wall, outward from the overhang. Drawing a deep breath, she thrust the cloak's edge between her lips and bit down fiercely on it. That she dared not lose. Then she extended her arms and hands as far as she could upward.

Zass had left her shoulder and was up there again with the alien. Simsa both saw and felt those claws close about her wrists, even as she had half feared that they would.

4

She was wafted aloft as easily as if she wore one of those gravity-nullifying cubes Thom had used during their exploration of the forgotten city in which she had found her other self. But this wafting was by no machine—rather through the strength of the rock dweller who slipped back into the shadowed window hole even as Simsa was drawn upward, so that when the grip was released she stood on her own two feet inside a dusky hollow. There was a faint light which issued not from any crack in the rock walls now closing about her, but from the body of the creature who had brought her here.

It stood taller than she—perhaps able to match height with the untrustworthy officer on the spacer. There appeared to be no neck. The round ball of the head, with the still clicking mandibles and the huge eyes, sat directly on its rounded upper torso. That was a well-stuffed oval of the plush fur connected to the lower portion of the thing's body by an

53

overly narrow waist. The lower portion of the body was nearly twice the length of the upper and banded across the fur by stripes of a darker shade. The hind legs were the most strange of all. They were very long and powerful and, when the alien squatted back on the middle joints of the appendages, they reached above that thin waist. Like the upper "arms," these bore no masking fur, only two rows of spikes erect and as menacing-looking as the claws which scratched the floor when it moved a fraction. The bottom of the lower portion of the body also touched the floor, apparently giving the stranger balance.

Zass had been flying in circles; now the zorsal settled down once again on Simsa's shoulder, claws digging painfully into the girl's skin. Bending her head closer, Zass rubbed cheek with Simsa.

"What do you?"

An abrupt question delivered with a sense of impatience. The girl looked around at the zorsal and then at the waiting monstrosity. It was plain that they could communicate after a fashion, but only through the aid of Zass. For when she tried with all her might to center thought toward the waiting stranger, Simsa received nothing in return but a sickening, whirling sensation which made her close her eyes for a moment and hold on tightly to that which was real—that she stood here with Zass and that—that—thing and was not tossing elsewhere in a place that had no safe anchor.

"I run," she returned, simply because she felt that only the absolute truth was possible with this one. Zass could pick her thought out from her words, or her head, but enough of the old Simsa remained that she must speak aloud in order to hold on to reality at all.

"What runs behind?" At least the answering message relayed through the zorsal was logical.

What did run, in truth? Perhaps the officer from the ship she had fled, perhaps another of his humanoid species. But mainly, Simsa knew at that moment, she ran not from any person or living thing, but because of her own fear—her own determination that she would remain free within as well as without herself.

She could never free herself now from the Elder One. That she had faced and admitted. At first she had been welcoming, aflame that she had found something, a part of her that had been lacking all her life and that she must have. Then she had realized that to this new inner dweller there must follow a surrender of that other Simsa whom she knew the better. Free? Inner freedom she could not control, but freedom without she could.

"I do not know." Again it was the truth which that other drew from her.

There was no expression readable to human eyes on the big-eyed round of the greenish furred face. She would not try again to reach the other by straight thought. However, she did aim a question of her own, determined somehow to keep a kind of parity with the alien, not to be as a small child answering questions of an Elder.

"Who are you?" She tried to make that emphatic, hardly knowing how it might reach the other through the filter of the zorsal's skittery thoughts.

"Fear."

For a long startled moment Simsa thought that that other had also answered simply, and with a threat. Then the rest of it, fading in mind touch but still understandable, came through:

"You fear—" It would seem that the other was simply going to ignore Simsa's demand. "There is a right to fear—"

Again Simsa was startled, startled this time into jerking back a space and throwing out the hand that held the rod as a barrier against a wriggling blot struggling freely in space before her.

One of the sand swimmers in all its slimy ugliness, so real that she was almost certain she could touch and feel the soft pulpy body. Then, as instantly as it had made its appearance, it winked out. Hallucinations! Even as the sand swimmer itself had used that talent against her.

"You fear—" Again the words squeezed past her amazement to deliver their message.

No yellow blob this time. There was—the figure was not as clear cut or as well materialized—perhaps it was too strange and alien to this other that it could not be fashioned sharply. But nonetheless she looked at a ship's officer.

"It is strange." That was conveyed to her although the thoughts coming through the zorsal had no expression of bewilderment. "This one—your kind?"

Simsa shook her head vigorously. "No kin." How that definition would fare in Zass's receptive thought she could not tell. The zorsals were mainly loners after they reached their second year, their mating being a hurried affair, immediately after which they separated, one sex from the other.

The tenuous form of the space officer did not blink out so quickly. It might be that the alien was either trying to refine it into better detail or was comparing it closely with Simsa to refute her own quick denial that it was like herself.

"What do you?" The first question of all was repeated.

Simsa took a deep breath. She would be guessing, but she

believed that this creature wanted from her a deeper reason for her flight—for her fear—not just what had set her wandering across the stone-clad landscape.

"I have—power." She cupped both hands about the rod of her power staff and held it a little out from her body. "He—wants that power."

The light that came from the alien body flared as much as if it held one of the lights Thom had carried months ago, much plainer and sharper than a torch.

And, in answer, for she had certainly not called upon any of the skill of the Elder One, the moon horns, the sun set between them, flashed into life also, giving off a radiance that warmed Simsa's body where it reflected that gleam from her black skin. Once more she felt her hair stir and guessed the ends of it were rising. But this time there was no feeling of being drained. No, she was pulling strength from without, not from depths within her.

The glow of the alien's body faded into a faint sheen, almost flickered. Now the life in the rod was withdrawing also, but still not outward but inward so that she no longer felt any lack in her body. Simsa might have eaten well, drunk deep, slept soft. She was completely restored in her inner strength.

"You—have—the not-haze—" Zorsal folded her wings, shifting from one foot to the other on Simsa's shoulder. The girl was not sure what was meant by that. Then one of the long spined "arms" moved at the center point, flailing forward, the claw at the end indicating without any mistake the rod.

Simsa clutched her treasure a little tighter. Was the alien striving to take her one weapon? But the claws did not quite touch the horned disc at the end, only held so for a few breaths, as if the creature were in some odd way measuring it. The joint creaked again and once more the long arm folded back as might that of an insect of her own home world.

The creature hitched around somewhat awkwardly, using that pointed end of its abdomen as a pivot. It did not turn its head to look at her again, but the order came clear enough from Zass:

"Come!"

The front appendages dropped to floor level and the back ones moved apart, giving the alien a strange likeness to an animal keeping its head down to sniff out a trail. The upstanding antennae smoothed backward, their tips well down on the wearer's back. The alien no longer moved jerkily, even though its posture made it appear so, and it moved rather swiftly. Simsa, lingering only to gird up the folds of the cloak knotted about her middle, had to trot in order to keep up.

There was no light except that subdued lumination that came from the large furred body before her. They had entered a tunnel through the rock, smooth of wall and floor, slanting downward after a few more swift strides, so that Simsa had to move with caution for fear of a stumble, the clawed feet of her guide apparently finding this surface less slick than it looked to the girl.

At spaced intervals there were other openings, but, though she peered into each as they passed, Simsa could see nothing. Therein the darkness was complete.

The gradual curve of the descending way became steeper, and Simsa tried to find, first on one wall and then the other, some manner of handhold to which she might cling if she slipped. She was about to appeal to her guide when she was aware of a splotch of brighter radiance on the floor. Before she could step aside her foot pressed a thick stuff which clung, even when she stepped, almost leaped, ahead.

When she planted the light-smeared foot again she found that her skin clung to the stone and steadied her, yet it yielded easily enough when she would move forward. Then she noted that a second large drop oozed from the thick body before her. For a moment she was revolted and would have tried to wipe the first coating from her foot with an edge of the cloak, but then, as if Zass had told her, she knew that this was not waste from the body ahead, but a gift meant to aid her.

Sure enough, as the creature deposited a third and final discharge, it turned and thrust its foreclaws deep into the mass, drawing them forth brightly shining. Then it flung these out to both walls, where they caught and held. The alien doubled its body in upon itself as if it were deliberately striving to break its own narrow waist, to bring chest and abdomen together, then hurled itself forward, the clawed forearms outheld to catch at something ahead.

A few steps farther on the floor vanished in a great hole as dark as any of the doorways they had passed. Simsa gasped. The rock dweller had swung across with the ease of one long accustomed to such feats, but she could not follow.

Or—could she?

Light blazed up beyond and she saw the alien waiting at the far edge of that trap. That increase of light displayed to Simsa against the left wall a ledge, so narrow that only if one turned one's head against the rock and squeezed along its surface could one pass that way.

The girl made sure that her cloak was knotted as securely as possible with the power rod in its fold still pressing warmly against her flesh. She studied the toehold path, liking nothing she could see of it, before taking a first cautious step forward. Perhaps it would have been easier to face the wall and not the abyss as she made her hesitant way onward. Except that a stubborn core of the Burrows Simsa was determined to look at danger in all its blackness, not to turn her back upon it.

She had no way of telling how deep that hole was. It appeared utterly black. The alien and Zass, who had already winged to the other side, were quiet; thus the dark was also silent except for her own breathing, which was in time with the fast beating of her heart.

That black hole so near her feet seemed to have a power of drawing her, so that she scrambled with outstretched arms on either side trying to find some hold, no matter how tiny, to sustain her. Thus she inched along. She was near enough to the far side where her two companions waited to feel the beginning of relief when the silence was broken by a sound. As if in the depths of that blackness something stirred— perhaps a creature winged as Zass but greater in size, beating those wings, about to take to the air.

Zass responded with a squawk that Simsa readily identi- fied. It was not surprise—rather fear. Yet the zorsal did not fly away but, on the floor of the farther side of the hole, jigged from one foot to the other, its mouth a little open, still uttering no sound. The alien creature which had been her guide this far raised one of those long jointed arms in a quick beckoning gesture, urging the girl to hurry. Simsa, her head snapping around so that she faced that well of darkness and what might move in its depths, slipped along one foot and then the other. The anchoring substance that the creature had exuded was wearing thin. She was losing her sense of being firmly rooted each time she put her weight fully on one leg so that she might either extend the other or draw it to her. Below, that sound grew louder. She could imagine wings stepping up action—some grotesque horror about to climb the air—for there was a distinct upper-reaching current from the hole.

Two more steps—

Zass gave tongue at last, a screech that meant defiant warning. The black in the hole appeared to possess more density, but the girl could not be sure whether she saw with her eyes or in a picture raised by fear to unnerve her just as she was so close to steady footing. Certainly there was movement from below, and she could see a kind of circling in the dark which was not unlike the whirling of the sand stream when those horrors that dwelt within it were minded to seek the world beyond.

She clamped her teeth hard, refusing to be panicked into a misstep now to carry her down into—that!

One step. She brought up her eyes, refusing now to watch. The movement of dark within dark reached her as a sick giddiness. Instead she forced her head around again and eyed the goal toward which she edged.

Out of the hole arose what looked like the spray of a fountain. Was it liquid or a reddish light formed of so many brilliant sparks that it could well seem a liquid? Against all her determined will, Simsa's attention was drawn to it. Like the whirling of the dark that appeared to give it birth, it caught and held the eyes—drew—

Pain, so sharp, so intense that Simsa could not suppress a choking cry following upon its first throb. On her bare right arm was a wink of light, a drop, a spark, of that which was playing higher and higher, spreading out farther and farther to encompass the whole of the dark well.

She caught her breath in a second sob, and, with one of the greatest efforts she had ever made, tore her gaze from the enchantment of that fountain and took the final step which brought her to the safety of the tunnel floor. But she slipped and began to topple back into the column of silver-red flame.

Once more those claws locked on her flesh, this time on one shoulder, sliding her along the floor, her flesh scraped raw by the harsh stone. On her arm that spark still lived and ate into her flesh viciously.

Beside her on one side squatted Zass, her wings fanning, uttering small mewling cries of distress. On her left settled the ponderous green body. The claw passed from her shoulder to the wrist of her painful arm. That was drawn upward even as the alien crouched yet lower. Then the girl felt the scraping of those mandibles across her skin and she shuddered in spite of the pain that already bit into her. That touch repelled her as much as if one of the tentacles of a river dweller had grasped her. A liquid flooded the place where the spark clung, and drops of a strong-smelling gel ran sluggishly down her forearm from the point of claw contact.

The angry fire in the spark was quenched, though Simsa felt still an ache such as a bad bruise might well leave. The claw grasp loosened and Simsa swiftly withdrew her arm. Although this touch had been for her benefit, and she had no doubt of that, still the contact had brought distaste, even nausea.

She had no trouble seeing that the alien had left a gob of gel over the wound and that it was hardening, for she could feel the pull of it on her skin. Again the long, furless, doubled-jointed arm swung out, but not this time to grasp any part of her; rather, it struck her almost with the force of a blow, pushing her farther from the spouting fountain, on down this new portion of the corridor.

For a moment she sprawled from the vigor of that shove and then she raised from all fours to her feet and came halfway around. Zass, with a second croaking call, took to the air while the inhabitant of these ways, again on all fours, butted the side of its head against Simsa, sending the girl on. She received a fleeting message, far less clear than the others, yet warning enough.

What wrought now within the well could not yet be through with them, not if they lingered near that fiery fountain. Simsa began to run. Her large companion, for all the awkwardness of its person, moved with a swift glide that took it to the fore, until with an appearance of exasperation it snapped out, its mandibles catching the untidy ends of Simsa's cloak. There they held with the fierce might of a metal trap, so that the girl was drawn along at a speed to set her gasping.

They rounded a twisting turn in the tunnel and Simsa near lost her footing at that sharp pull which started her in another direction. Having left the light that the well fountain had given them when it streamed, Simsa could see only dark walls a little away as they passed, and those because of the emanation of the huge body beside her. There were more openings which they passed at racing speed, a second turn, and then ahead was light bright enough so that even at this distance it made Simsa blink. For the first time since she had begun her journey past the well she became aware of the warmth of the rod against her body.

That this thing of power had faded completely out of her mind during her escape from the fountain-thing broke in her thoughts as an unanswerable puzzle. Simsa of the Burrows had begun to believe the rod had no limits. Even the Elder One had not roused in her when the pain in her body had come as a warning. The intrusion of the Elder One into her mind, which she generally half resented, now completely surprised and frightened her by its absence. Simsa of the Burrows, the girl knew then, had been uppermost during that encounter. She had, from the first moment of finding her likeness and opening herself to that inanimate material which had held for so long, come to depend more and more upon the Elder One—to believe that she was invincible, to resent the knowledge held by her. Now this. Where was the Elder One, and why?

The alien bore her steadily along toward the distant light, and they emerged from the tunnel into a place so utterly different from the barren rock of this world that Simsa was astounded and could only stare and wonder.

This was not a desert land. If the great basin or hollow was indeed floored with rock, there was no sign of it. Growths certainly large enough to be termed trees were set in ordered rows, an opening—a path—between their ranks directly before the three from the tunnel. The boles were not too large; Simsa could probably have clasped arms about the nearest and interlocked fingers on the far side. In color they were a smooth bluish green, lacking the roughness of bark. But at a height to clear the round head of the alien, who now rose to sit as it had when it first confronted the girl, they branched thickly with fine stems which bore long ribbon leaves of blue, rippling continually, though Simsa could feel no hint of any breeze.

Behind these guardians of the path were masses of shorter foliage changing in color from a deep true blue, through green, to yellow. And those, too, rustled and trembled as if they provided hiding places for all manner of would-be ambushers. Zass gave a cry of triumph, soaring up and out to fly above the trees in the manner of her kind, and when Simsa's eyes followed her she saw an oddity about the sky. That haze that had prevailed over the rock land looked much thicker here, though more luminous, and the stifling heat of the outer world was tempered by many degrees.

The tree-guarded path ran straight, and even on it there was no hint of rock or sand, but rather a thick growth of what appeared to be very short-stemmed, thickly packed vegetation in patches of color, some yellow, some green, some blue, and here and there a showing of silver white. The farther the path ran, the taller grew the guardian trees. But those were not high enough to hide what was at the end of the way.

Like unto the rocky upcrops that walled in this oasis of vegetation, there stood a structure: a square cube of blue which shaded to green at its crest. And its green crest was patterned with evenly spaced windows or entrances open to the air with no suggestion of any barriers in the form of doors. Appearing at some of these were creatures that so well matched the one accompanying the girl that they could have been cloned. These took off from the openings in easy leaps, propelled by their heavy back legs. They might have been diving down into the mass of growth below them like swimmers entering a sea. Once they were swallowed up by the reach of tree and bush, they vanished completely from sight. None of them had appeared to notice the three who had come out of the dark rock ways.

Zass wheeled and turned, coming back to settle on Simsa's shoulder, rubbing her furred head against the girl's cheek.

"It is the place." The alien accented the explanation beamed through the zorsal by a jerky movement of a clawed forelimb.

"The place? What place?" Since that compelling hold had been lifted from her, Simsa had made no attempt to go farther into the open, to step upon the plant carpet of the road.

"The place of the nest." Zass's thought had, the girl decided, an impatient twinge, some emotion of the alien carried through. Perhaps to their guide this was like Kuxortal, so well known a landmark that the whole world should recognize it.

Having so answered her, the big green creature dropped once more to four feet and scuttled on. Nor did it look back when Simsa made no attempt to follow. She was curious, yes, but her caution had been triggered by the inhabitant of the sand stream, by the well, and certainly by the alien itself. That wariness which had served her so well as a nameless, kinless one in the Burrows came to the fore. Thus she deliberately squatted down on her heels, narrowly surveying all that lay before her. The one who had brought her here appeared to have forgotten her entirely and suddenly pushed with force between two of the tree trunks into the deep curtain of the foliage and was gone.

Simsa absently rubbed the fountain wound, where soreness still made itself felt. Under the touch of her fingers the jellied stuff stripped away, and she looked down to see there was not even the thin line of any hurt. On impulse she took up the rod in her two hands clasped together and let its head sway forward so that the horn of the moon pointed toward that building. There was no more coming or going at the high windows. It might have been deserted long since.

Without any willing or conscious movement on her part, the rod began to move. She stiffened her grasp, fighting to keep it still, and discovered that all her strength was not enough to bring it into the same position. The horns were above, they were below—they were this side and that—but Simsa for all her trying could not hold them in a line with the green-crested block.

She let the rod drop to her knees to think this out. The rod could draw upon power—it could transmit also the power within her. It was a weapon as well as a warning shield. Therefore—she attempted to reason carefully and coolly (as she would have done having found some mysterious thing buried back in the Burrows, something that would be worth much if she could only solve its purpose)—therefore, perhaps there was a defense here. But why? Was it—Simsa sat up straighter and her lips parted a little, her heart beat faster— was it that such as the Elder One had been known here in long-ago times, and that thus there had been good reason for the indwellers to learn how to withstand the power that Simsa could call upon?

Elder One—her thought was as sharp as a call—Elder One! Though she strove to throw down every defense, there came no answer this time. She was still the lesser—the Simsa of the Burrows, for all her rod and her jeweled trappings. She was—alone!

5

It was the needs of that third part of her, her body, that
broke through Simsa's absorption. Hunger and thirst at last
overcame such reviving effects as the rod had provided. She
surveyed the vegetation now with more than just an interest
in the fact that it existed at all. Searching the pocket within
her cloak, she found a half packet of survival wafers—thin
and tasteless stuff, meant to contain in the smallest possible
portions enough nourishment to keep a humanoid alive and
moving. There was no more of the precious water, only a
soaked area about the flask in the cloak to betray its loss.

Though Simsa in this lifetime had never before been off
her home world, she well knew from warnings aboard the
ship and from the stories of the space crew that, fair as a new
planet might be, any of its liquids or natural food might also
act as swift poison for the off-worlder.

She held a half wafer in her hand and it crumbled yet more

in this aridity. To attempt to eat that was to choke on dry crumbs. All this growth below argued that it must draw upon real water—and surely not some stream of moving sand.

She was aware that Zass had dropped out of sight, gone questing lower in the brush behind the trees. Hunger and thirst—answers to those were more important now for her continued existence, than thought-searching for a second self. Surely the Elder One had never been bound to one world in her own time—Simsa had too often caught hints of a wide-roving life before that one had chosen to wait in her own way for deliverance by a far descended female of her blood.

Simsa's lips quirked in a half smile. Let the Elder One sulk or haughtily withdraw. But somehow she was sure that were she to make some wrong choice, to endanger her body, there would be a speedy warning. This was a part of their unwilling partnership that she had never put to the test before.

Under her feet the splotches of mosslike vegetation that carpeted the roadway gave forth a sharp scent, but not an unpleasing one. The odor certainly had none of the rankness of the Burrows' ways, nor any warning stench such as the sand river had given. She walked forward with an outward air of confidence which she held to as she would have held the cloak had it been cooler here. As she turned her head from side to side, striving to pierce the wall of thick growth that twined and matted behind the tree columns, she could see no possible opening, no hint of any fruit or berry ripening there, certainly no sound or scent of water.

Into her mind thrust the raw triumph of Zass. Somewhere in that maze the zorsal must have made a kill, for only freshly slain prey could bring that particular involuntary instant of communication. Zass had killed, but what and where there was no answer. And, if the zorsal feasted on some form of life subject to the aliens—perhaps so much the worse for both of them.

Firmly she pushed the new stab of fear to one side. She had come close enough to the cube building to see that the only openings at all, on this side at least, were those at the edge of the roof. Between the ground and those was only a smooth wall. Perhaps the aliens with their own sticky body fluids could make such a climb with ease, but there was no such opportunity for her.

Simsa stood for a long moment, her head held high, her nostrils expanded to their full extent, as she turned very slowly about, testing each possible way. There were odors in plenty—none of them obnoxious, some close to the perfume of flowers. Then—water!

She had heard that certain off-worlders could not scent water, though all of the lesser life-forms could. Evil-smelling as the Burrows were, one must for very life's sake cultivate an inward listing of odors in defense. There was water, not of the sea as it might have been back on Kuxortal, but rather stream clear—in that direction!

There was also no opening in the brush and she could not soar above its curtain in Zass's way. Simsa worked with her blanket cloak—there were thorns on brush stems, she had seen that from the first. What protection she could give herself she would. She had already frayed and pulled a hole in the middle, now she let her head slip through and the other folds she draped about her, flipping the ends up to cover her arms.

Then, rod in hand as a tool to hold back the entangling sprays of leaf-covered vine or branch, she advanced into that wilderness. As she took her first steps, trying to hold aside what was too thorny to break and throw from her path, Simsa was at once aware of the rustling which was brought about by no wind. Only the branches and leaves were aflutter, the disturbance directly before her. It was as if these rooted plants and trees were communicating one with the other, resenting her coming, urging each other to a stiffer defense.

With her cloak covering held by a thicket of thorn branches, Simsa was brought to a halt. One such swinging stem, as thick as her forefinger, looped down before she could dodge and caught in her hair, its movement not concluded until the silver strands were well entangled. Now she could not even move her head without an answer of sharp pain from her scalp. She had seen insects so captured by sticky cords produced and woven by creatures much smaller than their prey. Only here it was the vegetation to which she was prisoner.

Sharp pain in one cheek followed the flailing of another thorned tip, and her cloak, which she had planned as protection, became her downfall. Something seized its folds so tightly that even were her hair unentangled she could not have slipped free. The girl pursed her lips and whistled. Zass had found prey, she must have escaped this trap, therefore—

Only, before she heard any flapping of wings, there came again that sound which had saved her in the rock desert. The mist over this basin valley—she could only see a fragmented portion of it, her head held as it was now—was thicker than the haze above the desert. Not even a shadow showed through its padding of what should be open sky. Yet above that, sounding very near now, came the throb of a flitter's passage. Nor was it only bound across the valley. . . . Simsa thought that from the continued sound it was circling.

Persona signals—from the first she had thought that perhaps without her knowledge she might be carrying a direction clue for hunters. To her, many of the machines of the spacepeople approached magic. And always it was machines that served them so. During her imprisonment on the ship, she might well have been subjected to a scanning, some strange and terrifying treatment that imprinted her scent, her person, the cast of her thinking mind, upon one of those machines.

One thing for this moment was more important than a possible captor out of sight above. The branches that had so efficiently captured her became motionless at the first sound of that off-world ship. A moment later they went into quick and painful action. She was literally dragged forward; the clutches in her snarled hair used to pull her were enough to bring tears of pain to her eyes. Though she tried hard to free herself, flailing about with the rod, that action won her nothing but bleeding scratches, some of them so deep as to be close to wounds.

She could not see how those clutches on her hair and her body were transferred from one bush to the next, but somehow that happened. She was sure that bits of her hair, together with her scalp, were left behind. Blood dripped down her face. She could taste it as it touched her lips. Still the bush tore as one growth sent her stumbling to the next. Their rustling was a buzzing in her ears which seemed even to go deeper—into her very head, stirring her thoughts into wild panic.

Attack from creatures one could understand, but to have plants rise up against one was a kind of madness. Inside she cowered and tried hard to fight her fear. Then she was whirled, gasping, bloodied by scratches, half-deafened by the rustling, into an open space. Open as to the ground, but here were trees in a circle. Their branches met and interlaced over her head so that she could no longer view the haze. Though still, now that she was free of the side growth, she heard the flitter—the beat of its return growing louder as it seemed to head for the space just above the trees now roofing her in.

Simsa tripped and fell, the last of the brush having handled her so fiercely, and hit hard against stone. However, this was not the rock of the outer desert lands, rather a coarse gravel which skinned and pocked her knees and the palms of her hands. It was of a bright orange color, and it helped to make a setting for what was undoubtedly a pool.

There was also the play of a fountain—though not one of fiery particles such as had arisen in the well of the tunnel. Rather this leapt and then cascaded back into a wide, shallow basin, the heart of which was carven stone in the form of three loops, the center one footed between the sides of the other and wider two. Around the basin came a pattering of smaller feet on the loose gravel, and Simsa faced her errant zorsal, who, by the dampness of her fur, had been sporting in the water.

Simsa crawled to the pool side to plunge both of her scratched and smarting arms into the liquid. It had not the clarity she associated with the water she knew, being faintly green, but the scent!

She cupped her hands and scooped up what she could, to drink and drink again. This water, if water it was, tasted like the potent wine old Ferwar had kept jealously for her own comfort on the wet and cold days of the leafless season. It was strength itself as she swallowed and felt it within her throat, somehow both comfortingly warm and refreshingly cool. Before she drank for the third time, she bathed her face. Those scratches burned with renewed fire for only an instant or two, and then the pain was gone, and she could see in her reflection that even the most wicked of those tears in her skin appeared to have closed. Such comfort she had been able in the past to summon—or the Elder One had done—from the rod. Here, where nature was cruel, there seemed to be other kindness.

She was still bathing her throat and shoulders when the same brush that had used her so badly swung all to one side, without any forcing pull that Simsa could detect. Through the opening so made there came the alien, or an alien. At least it resembled to the last hair of its antennae, as far as she could detect, the one who had brought her here.

The creature halted beyond the edge of the basin, facing her across the play of the water. Zass, who had been paddling with both front paws in the fountain spray, gave a leap and flutter of wings to reach Simsa's shoulder.

"These . . . are your hunters?" The alien did not glance upward at the sound's source, which at that moment seemed directly overhead. "Or have you called them?"

The words dropped clear and cold from Zass's thought to hers. Simsa believed there was an aura of menace about them. Words could deceive if the one who uttered them was clever enough, but thoughts . . . If they could only speak directly without the shifting through the zorsal!

Moved by some inner push that Simsa had no time to explore, she sat cross-legged on the gravel and thrust the smooth end of her rod into the loose stuff. When it was rooted firmly she slid her fingers up, tilting the tips of the

horns in the direction of the other, and, not now beaming
directly to the zorsal as she had before, she began to present
what she wanted to communicate as shortly and clearly as
possible—pausing now and then to try and order her thoughts.

Her reason for escape from the spaceship, with no choice
of a landing save such as the equipment of the Life Boat
offered, her travel across the waste of rock, the battle with
the sand-stream horrors—

As she marshaled all these into proper sequence, she strove
to picture in her mind those actions and beliefs that were
concrete, together with the nebulous things that were her own
guesses, colored by her emotions. After all, she had no
suspicion of that space officer, of the medic, that she could
prove true. Though she herself was convinced that the fear
that drove her from the galactic voyaging ship had very real
roots.

If she were reaching the alien in this way, and not through
Zass, she had no evidence of success. But she was startled
out of her concentration when she saw issuing from the brush
and coming into the clearing of the fountain more of the
green-furred creatures—at first glance complete duplicates of
the one who had brought her into the valley. Their great
faceted eyes centered on her and they squatted down, their
large knees near up to the level of their heads—a silent and,
to her, a disturbing circle, so that now her thought stream
faltered and she held to sending by all the force her will
could summon.

It was completely silent. Even Zass huddled down voice-
less—quiet except for the buzz of the searcher in the air,
whose passing sound grew stronger, then faded in a regular

pattern. The flitterer must be circling, that circle growing the tighter with each passage.

Remembering what she had seen of the valley from the mouth of the tunnel, Simsa believed there was no cleared space wide enough to let the other-world carrier ground. Why did it remain above? Perhaps it was broadcasting directions for search to a party on foot.

"What have you that these want?" That demand was sharp and clear, and it had not come through Zass. She—or rather this other—had made contact at last directly with her.

"It is what I am." Simsa stirred. The rod was warming in her hand. The Elder One who had withdrawn, leaving her alone as she had always been to fight this battle; surely she awoke again. Even more slowly and with greater effort Simsa launched into the time before she had been escorted aboard the spaceship ("honored guest" they had been too quick to tell her, but her senses, honed to a fine edge in the always perilous Burrows, had answered "captive").

Was this big-eyed nonhumanoid really able to catch and understand her tale? How much contact had this barren world ever had with spacecraft and those who flew from world to world? Might the whole concept be wild fancy in their minds?

There flashed into her thoughts now not the pictures she had been fumbling with, trying to build, but something else—a holding to her conceptions she did not understand at all. No! Simsa of the Burrows screamed noiselessly. She was being fast pushed into an impotent captivity once more. Each time the Elder One returned was with stronger hold, more in control. Simsa shook her head from side to side as if she were threatened by a winged creature flying for her eyes, her mouth, to attack. Only the attack was in her head—not without—and she could not so loosen the will of that other.

The flicker of truly alien thought was like a flashing light shone brutally into her eyes. She thought she saw fragments of strange pictures. Buildings stood and were gone in an instant; shapes that moved and might be either intelligent beings or threatening animals rose and vanished in the space of a breath. It was like listening to a speech one should be able to understand but was spoken so swiftly that thought could not translate word.

Now the rod was bending in her hands, making her battle for mastery over a length of metal. Only for a fraction out of time could she put up a show of defiance. Then her hands no longer obeyed her. The rod was inverted so that the points of the horns touched, bit into the gravel. Her fingers were under the control of that other one and with their support the horns dipped, pushed away, came back—swung to this side and that.

There were loose markings in the gravel now, half-seen patterns. Then five of the aliens were leaning forward, their eyes no longer holding Simsa's gaze but fast upon that which the horn left as it moved. Also she could read that message, almost—though it caused sharp pain between her eyes when she attempted to hold those lines in sight and think of them.

Then—there was no trouble at all. What the rod of power had so drawn was a symbol of power, one from the far, far past. It was a mark of identity, a request for aid, a warning. Each small, stark line could have more than one meaning, and some such she could only inscribe because time beyond time had always made them so.

One of the aliens, not the one who Simsa believed had

been her guide, moved around the edge of the fountain to squat opposite the girl, studying the lines. A hand claw swung out to alter two rays of the pattern in a modifying way. Then mouth mandibles sent up a loud clicking and two of the others thrust back into the brush and were gone.

The one who had recognized the pattern now began to gesture with its claws, opening them to their greatest extent, bringing them together with a rattling snap. Dimly Simsa recognized a rhythm in that crackle of horn-covered flesh. Not speech, something else, more powerful than words. Perhaps even a weapon.

She who was now in command of the girl's body brought the rod back so that the horns touched her breasts. Through her body began a humming vibration which rose steadily until Simsa of the Burrows knew fear. Something had awakened in her to answer the claw-clicking. Humming linked with click. No, that vibration, she knew now, was not aimed at her body. It was fortifying whatever powers had been loosened and—waited.

Part of her answered the click and hum, but another bit of her, Simsa of the Burrows loosed for this duty alone, listened for another sound—the buzz of the off-world flyer. Surely it was louder again!

The clicking claws moved faster and faster, advanced out over the pattern. In her own grasp the horned rod dropped forward once more pointing at that stretch of earth on which that design had been set.

And—the earth began to move. Even as the sand had fountained up to emit the many legged horror of the stream, so did an ever-lengthening rope of the gravel arise, thicken, take on solid form. It spiraled up and up, although Simsa could not raise her head to watch it. That other held her solidly prisoner, eyes upon the rooting of that column in the pattern.

All the lines of the pattern had now disappeared, disturbed, pulled into the being that was growing. Toward the pillar flashed water from the basin, combining with the earth and gravel, licking quickly up and around, binding the other into a truly solid shape—not unlike the tentacle of a sand beast, yet already far beyond such in length of reach.

The alien had shoved back from the column, which drew more and more of the earth's substance into it. Simsa followed, rising to her feet. That spinning length was thicker than any of the trees about them, and still it grew, faster to reach above, but always adding to its girth as it went.

The color was changing now. Having pulled the gray-brown gravel into it, it was adding to its substance earth from below that covering, and to that dull brown were streaming torn leaves from the brush, longer ones from the trees. Still it spun as now there came from its core a growl which deepened as the reaching spout became thicker and taller.

Zass was on Simsa's shoulder, her talons clamped tight as if she feared that she also would go flying to make a part of that force-born column. The roar reached into Simsa even as the hum, the clatter of the claws had done earlier. She could no longer see the alien or the others who had been there. The solid stem of the growth cut them off.

There was a last high note of protest, perhaps the earth of the valley crying against the loss of its covering. Then the column whirled loose from its rooting, spiraled up as straight as a well-cast spear into the air.

Simsa discovered now that she could watch it going, her

head well back. The tip of it had already vanished into the haze, the rest and thicker part of it fast following. And the sound it still made was the roar of a storm-born tempest. Out and out—

The Elder One was too exhausted by whatever had been wrought here to hold her other self longer in check. Though the girl had no idea what had been done, yet she found herself listening with some eagerness for the sound of the flitter, if such could ever break through the whoop of the storm wind.

What had they wrought? A thickening of the natural roofing over the valley rendering it even more opaque? Or something else?

She could see no difference in the haze. Instead there grew in her a certainty that what had been born here was no defense, but a weapon aimed at those who searched. Sturdy as a flitter was, there could be danger from wind, sand, a whirlpool in the air.

Simsa's teeth closed upon her lower lip. Had she not wanted escape? Could she, with her so small influence over what—or who—dwelt in her, dictate what kind of escape? Yet she shuddered now, and not from the demands of the power. She could see, impressed against the veiling of haze, a picture that might be all too true: a small craft caught in the fury of earth and air, crushed, downed, buried even as it fell, and with it humanoids, perhaps not kin, yet—

Thom—his face flashed over the scene of the struggling, doomed ship. They had stood shoulder to shoulder once. If he had not delivered her into the hands of those others with their ever-demanding quest for knowledge, if he had foreseen . . . She was not certain, she had never been, in truth, that he had betrayed her knowingly—only without thought, because to him she was a treasure. Thom—

The smooth-faced off-worlder about whom she had built up so much resentment, had dismissed as useless in her own struggle for freedom from the system he had been so eager to serve—she could see him now.

She could see him now!

There was only that face on the underside of the haze through which the swirling pillar had completely disappeared. But she could see Thom. His eyes, set obliquely in a face where the flesh was so much lighter than her own, were closed. The mouth which had been always so firmly held was gaping a little, and from the gape ran a dark trickle. There was no life in that face.

Thom dead? To the Elder One, his vanishing had meant little, but this Simsa had always clung to the hope that if she could reach Thom, in some manner he could point a way to her freedom—even though he might have thoughtlessly betrayed her in the beginning.

She stared as one confronted by such a horror as moved in the sand rivers. Then she broke—through the tight control of the Elder One, through whatever bonds that other and the alien had woven to do what they had done. If it had been Thom in that flitter, and that other part of her had killed him . . .

She did not care if the whole of an off-world ship had been blasted into nothingness—but Thom was a different matter.

"Zass!" The zorsal might not understand her words, though she had always answered to her name. "Thom! Seek!" And to the words she added the imperative mental command that could arouse the creature to action.

With a spring into the air, Zass took off, her skin-covered wings beating as she followed the whirling weapon of gravel up toward the haze—though she did not take the same path but rather headed out toward the north in a way that would lead her across the valley to the guarding cliffs. If Thom was out there—Zass was a hunter with talents no humanoid could equal.

As the zorsal flew, Simsa thrust the rod back into her girdle. It was no longer warm against her flesh—the power was gone, perhaps exhausted by the work it had done. Just as the Elder One was once more lapsing into the quiet that covered her when Simsa of now was free. She spoke to the green aliens directly and with the vigor that anger gave her. Someday she would learn the key—how to use the Elder One's knowledge without losing also that other person. Now she must make the most of the time in which she was free to be herself.

"What—happens—to—the—flyer?" She spaced her words, speaking them slowly and emphatically as if so she might project their meaning without Zass's translation.

There was no movement, no change in the two who were still with her. She could have ceased to exist for them. Both of them stood erect, their bodies at an awkward angle so that their heads were turned up toward the haze. There was still the whining of the whirlwind, but it was dying. And no buzz of flitter broke through it.

Simsa caught up her cloak and stalked around the pool where the spray that had fed the pillar was once more but a small play of water. In spite of her distaste she put out her hand and caught at the arm of the nearest of those watching.

She gave a hard jerk and the tower of green fur near toppled on her, the faceted eyes dropped to meet hers.

"What has happened?" demanded the girl, determined that the other would neither shake her off nor longer ignore her.

6

Above opened one of those squared apertures of the blue bulk of the building. Once back at home—"nest"—her companion shook off Simsa's clutch as easily as though the horn-smooth covering of the slender upper appendage had been greased, twitching even the spikes easily through the girl's fingers. Paying no attention at all now to Simsa, the other began to climb the wall—up to that gaping mouth or entrance. Though from the outer rim of the valley, she had seen much going and coming from these apertures, now they appeared blank, deserted.

Simsa sought holds for her own hands, but, to her groping fingers, the surface was smooth. The claws of the valley's inhabitants were more useful here than fingers could be. Zass? She could re-call the zorsal—but to what purpose?

She started to walk around the base of the huge cube. The

vegetation wreathed it for a space until bushes and trees made up a walling. But no entrance on this level appeared.

Taking a deep breath of resolve, the girl called—not aloud with the whistle that was Zass's own summons, but more awkwardly with her mind, sending out a need for help. As she did so she watched keenly the openings above. In none of those dark hollows did anything stir.

All right! So be it! She was left with only one chance—to return by the same underground way that had brought her here. Nor did she stop to wonder why this need drove her. There was safety here, of a sort, so why venture forth into the waterless rock world? Why?

Her hand smoothed the rod. This was what she had sought—freedom. The aliens had offered her no threat. They had indeed called upon the Elder One's skill to serve their own purpose. So well had they succeeded in that, that they might well look upon her as she looked upon Zass, a lesser life-form but a useful one.

If what they had summoned up had dealt with the flitter, as she guessed it must have, what should that matter to her? It only assured what she wanted—freedom from the off-worlders' avid curiosity, their desire to make of her a tool, one that she had no mind to be. Let well enough alone—that had always been Ferwar's own saying, drilled into her fosterling from childhood.

There remained Thom. They had fought as battle comrades, yes. But any debts between them had been canceled in full long ago. And it was Thom, was it not, who had drawn the attention of those beyond space to her own existence? She owed him nothing at all.

At the same time Simsa assured herself vigorously that this

was so, she swung around to face the clear road leading under the arch of the trees back to the tunnel mouth. Nor could she battle into surrender that in her which led her from one hesitating stride to a fuller one in that direction.

She had filled her water carrier at the fountain after she had bathed her scratched face. Now she noted that there dropped from the walling trees fruit, deep blue in color. Saliva filled her mouth at the thought of food as she picked up one that had fallen close enough to brush against her shoulder. To eat of this might mean death. However, the water had not poisoned her, but rather revived her, and she must have food.

Simsa broke the ovoid apart as she would a survival wafer. A golden pulp burst forth to sticky her fingers. She licked, first cautiously and then greedily, before she spit out a reddish pit. Now she avidly harvested a goodly store of windfalls, tying them into a corner of her cloak, as she headed toward the tunnel.

Even as the rich flesh of the fruit slid down her throat, she was thinking of that back trail. There would be no luminous guide this time—she must take the road completely in the dark. What of the pit where the fire-thing leaped? Without any light she could well tumble into that unwarned. To edge along the narrow path to safety a second time . . . Simsa swallowed and swallowed again, the soft fruit all of a sudden too much to easily get down.

This was folly—the worst of folly! For a Burrows-bred fosterling to risk all for a stranger! Twice her steps slowed, the second time at the very edge of the tunnel. She paused there to look back over her shoulder, for she had half hoped. But there was no stir at any of those openings. She was on her own. Was it because she wished to succor one of their enemies? Or could it be that they were very willing to have her no longer their concern—to see her dead in the barren land, perhaps, offering no threat to them at all?

Rubbing the fruit juice from her hands down the front of her cloak, Simsa took hold on the rod, facing into the dark of the tunnel way. She was using that thing of power as one blinded might use a cane tapping the way ahead.

She rounded the turn in the passage, half expecting to see before her the glow of that flame which had awakened at their coming here. It remained thickly dark. The Burrows had often been without any lights, nor did those who laired within them depend upon torches or lamps too freely—most of their errands had been solitary hunts which they had no intention of sharing with others.

Now Simsa drew upon memory—not that of the Elder One (she wanted no loosing of barrier there), but on what she had learned in this time if not on this nameless world. Unconsciously, because the habit had long been engrained in her by training, she was counting off steps. So many to that trap, then so many along the toehold at its side.

One hand for the tapping of the rod against the tunnel floor, one to the side so her fingertips slid along the wall. She gasped when those suddenly met with nothing, then remembered those many dark niches or doors that had been spaced along the corridor. Her head up, she also used what gift of scent she had. There was a musty odor which she associated with the passage itself, interwoven with the faintest trace of a metallic effusion such as she had always connected with the various machines of the off-worlders.

She slowed, stopped to wrap the cloak the tighter about

her, and then went to her hands and knees, creeping at hand-by-hand's length until her fingers met nothingness and she knew she had reached the pit.

Refusing to look down into the blackness lest she see that whirling which heralded the flame fountain, Simsa felt along the lip of the gap until she discovered that narrow ledge she had struggled across before. There was a stickiness which she stirred with thumb and forefinger, certainly the remains of that liquid emitted by the alien.

Simsa sat back on her heels. If she got across without arousing the danger below, if she found her way out onto the barren rocks, if . . . Her lips twisted and she spat several words well known to Burrowers, blistering in their meaning. Why? Who told her that this must be done? It was not the Elder One, she was too well aware of how that one could flash into command upon occasion. What set her to risk this? A vision on the haze of a man who was doubtless already dead? She was more than a fool—she was mind-twisted—and for the sake of her own kind she should have been eliminated long ago, as was done to any lacking in sense and reasoning power.

Still, even as she lashed herself so, she was certain that she could not retreat. From Thom, before those others had arrived at his call to take control, she had learned a great deal, not learning as the Elder One would measure it—though oddly enough in some things there were likenesses in acceptance of aid. Upon a strange world, when there was danger, off-worlders drew together—unless they were utterly mind-warped as had been those who had come to plunder on Kuxortal. She was no space-goer. And she had more to fear perhaps from off-worlders now than she had from the alien life. But it had been she, or a part of her, who had raised the thing she was sure had engulfed the flitter. And if Thom had been aboard . . .

Simsa thumped her forehead with the palm of her hand. Thoughts, why must she deal with thoughts? If she could not justify what she did, not to herself—so be it. She only knew that it was as if she once more hung from the compelling claws of the alien. She had no choice against these invisible claws that had come into being when she had seen Thom's face, perhaps his *dead* face, backed by the haze in the valley.

Hating what led her, but no longer fighting it, for there was no use in such a struggle, the girl got to her feet to begin edging along that narrow strip of walkway, the pit at her back, teeth set hard against lip as she strove to move without a sound to betray her.

What if the thing could not hear, rather sensed? She did not look over her shoulder, but scraped along the rock so that its surface abraded the cheek she kept to it as she moved. Without even viewing it, Simsa was aware that once again there was movement in the dark. Sweat ran down her face, smarted in the raw places on her skin. One step, another, this part of her memory was stubbornly blank. She had been too fearful before to reckon; now that same fear was rising in her like a smothering of her lungs, a choking in her throat.

On and on. In her own ears the beating of her heart was a drum for votive dancers, deep and calling, while breath came in shallow puffs. She would not linger. To stop moving was perhaps to anchor her immovably to await the torture of the spark fire to whip her down.

So far no light—she clung to the darkness which now meant safety. Step, hold, bring the other foot along. Again.

Again! Then she became aware of heat against her body. Even as the alien had a glow to light the way arising from her own frame, so did there arise radiance from the rod. Simsa could not spare the hand to tuck it farther out of sight. It was responding to power—to energy she could neither understand nor control.

She was certain, if she were able to look down, that that which lay in wait would respond. Step. Hold. Step. Sound now—a spitting such as might come from fat meat placed too close to a flame. Yes—there was brightness growing, not only between her body and the wall, but behind and below.

Light, enough to see!

Simsa hurled herself sidewise as well as forward, landing with bruising force on the tunnel floor. Behind her the infernal sparkling fire fountained upward a first questing tongue.

She turned her back on that growing brilliance and ran, half expecting it to launch an attack upon her, as had the thing from the sand river. Only speed was in the fore of her mind as she scuttled ahead.

It was light, far too light in the tunnel. Simsa gave a gasping cry as a spark swooped into her line of sight, seemed to strike straight at her, as might a well-aimed weapon loosed in fury. More sparks in the air, they touched and bit, leaving smarting if tiny hurts behind them.

Simsa fled on. There was other light ahead, faint but there. Still refusing to look behind, she panted into the room within the shell of the outer cliff into which the alien had first drawn her. Only then did she face about to see that, though they had not followed her into this rough-hewn chamber, there danced in the air of the tunnel she had just quitted a cloud of flame sparks, multiplying constantly. She had the frightening feeling that they were merely building up to collapse into a more solid flame—a creature that not even the Elder One could handle.

She threw herself at the window opening that had been her doorway. Scrambling up on the ledge, she swung over and dropped to the shelf where she had taken refuge before, then leaned against the rock, her breath coming in racking sobs. This was sheer panic such as had not gripped her since childhood. As she got her breath, Simsa could see that there were no sparks flying now from above. Since the heavier haze which was night on this world was tight drawn, those would have been instantly revealed.

She would not, could not, linger too near. Whether that which fed the sparks dared venture out of the dark well into the corridor, she had no way of knowing. Only she must put between its source and herself as much space as possible.

Thus, even as she had climbed there in her hunt for Zass, so did she now scramble down, fighting to remember so that she would miss no finger- or toehold. It was not until she had reached the foot of the cliff and looked up at the dark opening above that she was angered at her own fear. There were indeed those raw and smarting places on her skin to make plain the threat offered, but now she had a feeling that she had given way far too easily to what was more threat than attack.

Before her was that slowly flowing river of sand. She had crossed that with the bespelled cloak. Now she hunkered down on that carven place where a true bridge must once have been end-rooted. Sliding out of the cloak, she laid it flat on the stone, her flesh cooled by puffs of a wind that did not ripple the sand below but was becoming swiftly forceful.

Trying to beat her from her perch into the sand river? No! There was a danger in such a belief. Had it not been belief that had forged the bridge for her on this very place? She must not speculate, must keep closed those corners of her mind into which could intrude and be nourished the thought of dangers.

She ran one hand across the rumpled cloak, her fingers catching in the edge of the hole where she had torn a place for her head. Then upon it she laid the rod from her girdle. There was no warmth in it. There had not been since she had dropped from that window above. There could be tens of tens reasons why. The Elder One—

Simsa shook her head and grimaced. This she must do herself, for to loose that other one, to call upon her . . . That one might well have no sympathy for what Burrows Simsa was doing now. The Elder One would have no reason to succor any life she had helped to warn of. She might perhaps even try to extinguish it with her own power. Simsa of the Burrows must go forward now, and how she could do that?

She got wearily to her feet, tugged on the cloak again, swung the rod back and forth as if it were only a fishing spear. North or south? She had come in from the northeast when she had discovered this place. Surely the swirling sand flood could not cut it off entirely from the outer world—she had never heard of a stream that ran in a circle with no inlet or outlet.

South, then, for she had already made the journey along the northern way before she had found the bridge place. It would not be easy—but what had been on this world?

There was no "beach" along the edge above the sand river, nor would she have gone too close to what might climb

out of the water. Rather she continually climbed and descended a series of tumbled rocks or edged fearfully along
slides of gravel where a wrong step might send her spinning
down into that noxious flood.

Zass had not returned, and she had flown north when
leaving the valley. Therefore she herself might have a long
march back even if she could locate a crossing of the flood.
And she was tired. Night and day flowed so easily one into
the other on this world she had long ago lost all sense of time
as an exact measurement. But now her flesh and bones
measured for her. There was just so far she could force her
feet to carry her, and realizing that she was near the end of
endurance, Simsa dropped down behind a large boulder that
formed a small wall of its own, shutting her in so that she
need not watch the stream. She took a scant mouthful of
liquid from the flask she had filled at the fountain, ate two of
the sticky fruit. Then with the rod upon her breast as she had
slept ever since it had come into her hands, Simsa forced her
mind quiet, for she needed a clear mind and a rested body.
She walled fiercely away all thought of what might have
happened to the flitter and those within, and sought sleep.

Here where there was no rising sun one could truly see, no
cry of bird or buzz of insect to disturb slumber, she did not
know how long a time had passed before she wriggled in her
pocket of rock and wall and moved stiffly to sit up.

Those small burns the fire had left her all sprang to life.
She saw the spots of seared skin on her arms and hands, felt
them on her cheeks and throat. There was no healing from
the alien source this time; she shrugged and looked over the
edge of the rock that had sheltered her.

And there—she had been so close! A few steps more and

she might have— Simsa again shook her head at her thoughts. To have taken that path when she was so weary would have been folly. There were at least two places to pass that would require all her courage and strength.

At some time in the past there had been on the other side of the stream another outcropping of the blocklike rocks, not quite as tall as those to her right. There was very little regularity to that formation, so she could believe that it had not been shaped by intelligent endeavor to form an outpost for the valley defense—save that one corner to the east was acute- and regular-angled. The rest of it had been shattered. Some mighty blow had crushed the stone, crumbled it to a riven mass.

However, a portion of that mass had landed in the sand river, supplying an impediment where the thick stuff parted to flow, a narrower ribbon right below her perch, a wider one to the east. She could drop to that mass. The first of the streams was small enough to leap. The second one—let her reach it, and she could see better what was to be done!

She ate and drank sparingly, made sure that her supplies were as safe as she could make them. Then she descended to a rock where a center ridge afforded a precarious perch.

Did it offer enough of takeoff for a leap? And what of that gap farther on? She studied her possible landing and decided that the gap was better than her present perch. Working her way to the end of the ridge piece, she saw to the safety of her cloak, now twisted as tightly about her above her waist as she could manage. Also, she brought forth the rod and thrust it in twice to make sure that she would not lose it.

The rippling of the sand at the foot of her rock was steady, but Simsa would not allow herself to look. Instead, drawing upon the skills of her lean body, she jumped, landing only barely on the other rock, fighting desperately for hand- and footholds. Here she lay for a space, breathing fast and staring up into the haze. It was midday or later, and now she was conscious of the heat both of the air and of the rock beneath her.

Rolling over, she crawled on hands and knees to the other end of the rockfall and there surveyed the rest of the passage. This break was wider than the other portion of the stream and it had no good landing strip beyond. Simsa refused to accept that. There must be a way.

Looking higher, she picked out, partly shadowed by a tumble of rock, a darker spot, which, as she studied it, took on something of a likeness to the window holes in the fortress? home? city? behind her. Had she had about her all that she carried in the Burrows when about her nearly illegal business—a stout rope, with a small knife that opened into a grapple—the crossing would have been, perhaps not easy, but possible. But she was not equipped as in the old days.

Still, that thought held in her mind—a rope and a grapple. If the grapple held true, she could swing across above the surface of the sand, reach the narrow top of one of the tumbled rocks just below the suspected opening.

Simsa shed the cloak. The rod? It was too precious to risk. That left the metal strips of her kilt—which she had been so proud to assume and which she had since worn even when it would have been better not to in order to avoid attention. One strip still lay back beside that other river where she had been tempted to fish with such ill results. But with two—four more . . .

She speedily loosened a pair. They were limber in her

hold, not stiff, but they were also hard to bend, and she had to pound them against the rock with the help of a small stone until she had them entwined together, with two prongs pointed outward in opposite directions.

Rope? There could be only one source for that. Simsa now fell upon the cloak and tore a wide strip, or rather worried it loose with the edge of her grapple. Into this she fitted her small store of supplies—it would make a pack she could bind to her back. The rest of the tough material she tore, pulled, cut, and knotted into an unwieldy length of line perhaps half the width of her palm in thickness.

Knotting this to the improvised grapple, she again tested each and every knot. She was not depending upon illusion, or will, or power now, but on knowledge she had learned for herself, and that thought strengthened her determination to succeed. If she fell, she thought wryly, then that Elder One, with all her learning and skills, would end just as quickly as the beggar-thief out of the Burrows. Save that she was set on victory this time on her own.

It took three casts, even in the full light, to bring the grapple within that broken window place. Then Simsa threw all her weight backward, not just once but three times. Without realizing that she did so, she was mumbling one of the charms Ferwar had always sworn by and made her learn to summon fortune.

She was very careful in tying on her improvised pack, allowing herself two swallows of water. Her skin was slippery with sweat now and she deliberately rubbed her palms across the rock surface to pick up any grit that might adhere.

"Ready as I shall ever be!" She said that aloud stoutly as both a challenge and encouragement. Then, the awkward "rope" in her grasp, she cast herself directly into the hands of fortune by jumping from the end of her perch.

The swing of her rope took her only an arm's distance above the sand, and the force of her jump brought her up against a far rock with such a blow as nearly drove all the air from her lungs. But she held and began to climb, her feet braced against the riven face of the rock, her hands and arms cruelly strained. She reached the end of the rope, swung up one hand to hook over the edge where the grapple was fixed, and at last tumbled head forward into a cramped hollow where she merely lay, her breasts heaving from the struggle and the fear which, at the last moment, broke through the guards she had set.

She was safe across, and for a time that was all that counted. Her many bruises and scratches joined those earlier hurts, and she felt as if she wanted nothing but to lie where she was indefinitely. To be back on her pallet of rags in Ferwar's smelly burrow with a pot of fish stew and edible fungi boiling over the fire under the tending of her foster mother—that was sheer luxury. Why had fortune not granted that she remain so for her lifetime? She had meddled with things that were better left to slumber aeons longer. Now it was as if she were one of Lame Ham's people, made of sticks and rags, which he so skillfully used to summon up a crowd on market days while his partner Wulon plucked purses from the unwary.

This could be welcome sleep and a good dream. Yes, she was in no rock hollow, but underground, sheltered as always, where she had learned to be quick and clever and had few equals. There was Ferwar true enough; she need only put out her hand and she could clasp the edge of the old woman's outer cloak fashioned of patches upon patches.

"Ferwar?"

At her call the other swung around. Her face was very wrinkled and there was a difference in her eyes. She answered, with a zorsal's loudest scream.

7

··············
··············

"Zass!" Her own cry of recognition roused Simsa out of the deep exhaustion that had held her.

The zorsal perched on a point of broken wall well above the girl's head, nodding so that the stiffly held antennae were a misty pattern against the haze-shrouded sky. Zass was licking her paws with smug satisfaction, cleaning sticky patches from her claws and then her coat. The smell of overripe fruit reached Simsa, and she knew that her companion had been raiding those supplies she had brought out of the valley. Or had she? A quick glance at the bundle showed no change of wrapping. But Zass had the gift of wings—what did that lengthy journey through dark back to the valley mean to her?

Simsa whistled weakly. The zorsal paused in her leisurely toilet to look down. Her muzzle wrinkled, and her tongue shaped one of the low cries that the girl knew of old. Zass was very satisfied with herself. Now the small, furred body rose as the leathern wings unfurled and she flapped down to squat once again, this time beside the girl's body as Simsa fought bruises and stiff muscles to sit up.

Zass's self-satisfaction was familiar to Simsa. Just so did a zorsal signify a successful finish to any hunt. Then it was true—that last small doubt was gone. Thom was here, somewhere in this wilderness of barren rock, and Zass had found him.

The girl ate a little of the fruit, too, soft now, not far from spoilage under the glaring heat of this outer country, allowed herself sips of water. She offered some to Zass, but the zorsal refused it.

It was hard to reckon time, but the sky haze was darker close to the eastern horizon and brightest behind the tumbled rocks, the upstanding cubes. She had best be on her way. Simsa grimaced sourly as she got to her feet. Those burns from the tunnel's sparks, all the scrapes and bruises of her journey made themselves into small torments when she strove to stretch, to rub muscles in the calves of her legs which knotted painfully. As she shouldered the bag of supplies she spoke once more to Zass, trying at the same time to empty the fore of her mind of all but that face she had seen on the haze of the valley.

"Thom!"

Zass clapped her wings, producing a smacking sound which echoed among these rocks or ruins, whichever they might be, then took lazily to the air. She flapped about in a circle as Simsa worked her way out of that foreguardian of the valley world and trod once again the rock plain between cracked fissures. Having seen the girl so prepared to follow, Zass's flight straightened into a line pointing east yet, to Simsa's surprise, south. The girl had expected a northern pathway.

Nor did Zass keep to the air, but returned now and then to perch on the girl's shoulder and chitter what Simsa understood as complaints. Always the zorsal disliked any long march, since, winged, she could outfly those moving on the ground, and this was difficult ground to cover because of the constant breakage of the fissures. Sometimes it was necessary to detour for a space to get around one, and Simsa remained alert to any movement within, expecting at any moment to witness an upward surge of sand heralding the emergence of a monster. She swung the rod back and forth at waist level, always careful to point the horn tips toward any fissure she had to pass.

She was suddenly aware that the wind was coming in faster puffs than usual. Then her head came up with a jerk, and she faced directly into the lightest of breezes, still near furnace hot from the day.

Burning. Something burnt, and a stench of other odors that she had not breathed since she had left the foul agelessness of the Burrows. She moved the rod up and out. It was warmer in her hand. Another of the beasts about to attack?

Zass took off, her claw tips scouring Simsa's shoulder where there was no longer any protecting cloak. The zorsal angled even more to the right, heading over two large fissures and giving a loud squawking cry. Simsa began to run, though her way was a zigzag and not a straight path, to where the zorsal was again circling in a wheeling pattern of flight, continuing to give voice.

The other river! Simsa made herself slow lest she suddenly

skid over some lip of rock into that flood. What had Thom to do with rivers—such rivers as befouled this world?

She came upon disaster so warned, but still astounded. Zass had settled down—not on the rocky shore of the stream, but on a mass of broken metal which protruded out of the ripples of sand that must be tugging at it, though so far not able to swallow up the wreckage.

A flitter right enough, but one that looked as if a giant had caught the machine out of the sky and twisted it between his hands even as one might twist reeds to fashion a basket— only this had then been idly thrown aside. Marks on the rock showed where the flyer had skidded after a forceful landing, heading straight for the river which now held a good third of it in its thick grasp.

There were no signs of life about the cabin of the downed flitter. The rough, transparent, glasslike substance the off-worlders used to give vision but also withstand any attack of enemy or nature was so crackled that she could not see inside. The worst was that the skid that had taken it into the river had landed it against, and well up on, the far bank. Between Simsa and the wreck was a broad band of flowing sand.

The girl dropped her bundle and grimaced at being faced again by the problem of sand rivers and their hidden inhabitants. There was a chance that she could leap from the solid base of this shore to the top of the wreckage, but she did not know how well based the latter might be. She might land on a mass which would then simply tip her off into that muck which she had no intention of entering.

The zorsal was walking across the clouded upper portion, pausing now and then to lower her head and peer into a portion fairly clear of such veiling. Then she fanned her wings and sank her claws, extended as Simsa could see to their fullest reach, into one of the cracks, rising in a small jump with the aid of her wings while all four limbs were anchored in the shattered material.

A crackling answered her, and Zass bounced higher into the air, bearing with her a three-cornered fragment. With a series of splitting sounds, the rest of the badly broken window dome fell out and slipped down the tail of the flitter to cascade into the sand, where it speedily disappeared.

Simsa had no difficulty now in seeing bodies trapped in the wreckage; two of them, wearing the shining, one-piece uniforms of spacers, were wedged within. One had fallen forward, his or her head resting on unmoving knees. But it was the other Simsa saw and knew.

Her haze-borne vision in the valley was true. Thom, his head up and back, sat pinned there. His eyes were closed and there was that thin runnel of blood coming from the corner of his mouth. Dead?

On her hands and knees, lest she somehow lose balance and fall into the sand trap, the girl crept to the very edge of the cut in the rock that held the river, and tried to distinguish any signs of life. But he was too far away.

"Does—he—live?" She aimed her most urgent thought, adding to it all she had learned, at the zorsal, uncertain whether Zass could even pick up that question. Surely she knew the difference between life and death. Any hunter would. Simsa watched the zorsal alight again and move forward, with a strange caution. Zass might be approaching some trap which she must spring. With her hind claws caught in a pinch grip on the frame of the one-time viewplate, she folded her wings and swung head down, her front hand-feet widely spread apart.

A moment later those closed, one on either side of Thom's lolling head, and shifted it around a fraction while the zorsal studied the bleeding mouth, the closed eyes, with the experience of predator.

The sensation that was her answer reached Simsa just as the zorsal let go and moved over to test in the same way the other body.

Alive! But how badly hurt? And was that flitter equipped with the same help summoner as the Life Boat carried? Would it summon assistance in time from wherever this party had planeted? It might well be that all her solicitude was not needed, that already help was on the way, help Simsa had no intention of meeting.

The second one was dead—again an assured report from the zorsal. Zass had tugged the other's head up, and Simsa saw that this was that woman whose mind she had touched only to be revolted and frightened. This was that one who would seek out secrets with a knife, or by machines that would maim and kill! Knowledge so sought was debased and vile. Before she thought, Simsa followed the customs of the Burrows and spat as she would have into the footprints of one upon whom she called ill fortune.

But there was no need for that. The ill fortune of her own kind—the fortune they believed the worst—had already struck.

Her own kind? Simsa straightened and clutched the rod as if to turn it on herself. No! Not now—but there were no barriers that she could hold for long against that moving inside her. Out of hiding, or the resting place into which she had retreated after she had worked her power, the Elder One was again emerging.

There was already that slight shift in Simsa's sight. Some things sharpened, others faded as if there dwelt in her now another range of vision. Yet when she looked at Thom she knew that this was a task from which she would not be allowed to turn, even if she wanted to—that that broken body set just out of her reach had importance not only to Simsa of the Burrows, but also to her who co-dwelt within.

Zass loosened her hold on the woman, allowing the dead to crumple back. The zorsal did not have the strength or means to free the spaceman—that would lie with Simsa. And the Elder One—by all means the Elder One!

It seemed to Simsa, even as she yielded once more to the other, that each time she did so the Elder One grew stronger, more ready to take command. Only, having once begun the withdrawal of herself, she had always known she could no longer withstand the other.

What could the Elder One do here that Simsa could not? Build a bridge? Of what? The cloak was shredded. And Simsa would not go down into that flood of sand and what it must conceal to reach the broken flyer.

The zorsal had returned to Thom, settling on the edge of the frame that had enclosed the broken transparent bubble, and once more set her foreclaws again expertly to cradle the unconscious spaceman's head. This time she turned it cautiously so that his closed eyes were directly facing Simsa. Having adjusted the hold to her satisfaction, Zass raised her own head and gave a chirrup which was a bid for attention.

In Simsa's hand the rod moved, or rather the Elder One moved it. There came a beam of light, green blue—rippling as if it spouted from a fountain, narrowing until the ray appeared solid in its intensity. It struck directly above and between those closed eyes.

So it was held steady, not by Simsa's will but by that other's. The knowledge of what was happening was not shared. Simsa could only guess that this was meant to benefit. Then that beam flashed off as speedily as it had first shown.

Now it returned to alter target, striking upon the wreckage itself. No narrow beam now, rather a new kind of haze, puffing forth to envelop the whole of the broken flitter, encasing it, growing ever more dense. Simsa, who must stand by and watch while the Elder One was in command, uttered a cry.

The wreck, which was now but a black shadow within the haze the rod had engendered, slid away from the other bank, dropping its crumpled nose into the sand river. Yet the girl was certain that the Elder One had no mind to lose Thom. Why then let him fall into the hidden territory of the slime blobs?

The haze thickened below, thinned above. The broken observation bubble was nearly clear, while the underpinning was hidden. Yet still it moved.

It moved, and, within her, there came in answer such a draining of energy and life as she had never known, even when the Elder One had ruthlessly used her to some purpose such as the releasing of the valley whirlwind. There was no way to fight, to protect herself—she could only give and give.

Having woven its web of haze, the rod flipped back against her breasts and again Simsa cried out—this time in pain, for it might have been a glowing brand held forcibly to her skin. Nothing drifted or spun from the horns now. And there was nothing left within her to give. What the Elder One had wrought exhausted her. She fell upon her knees, the rod dropping from her grasp as she braced herself with both hands and straightened arms to keep from crashing headlong on the rock.

There was an impatience rising in her now—not borne from her own thoughts or desires, but out of the wishes of the Elder One. It would seem that she found this Simsa too frail, too feeble—

While the haze-enclosed wreck was down across the river now, it had not dipped into it as she had expected it to do, rather seemed supported by the haze upon the surface of the flowing sand. However, as she watched, the even flow of the sand was troubled by a dimpling of its surface; small hillocks broke out of the flow. And from these grew, like upside-down roots of hideous and poisonous plants, the weaving yellow tentacles of the blobs, small at first but spreading ever larger, longer.

It would seem, however, that the rod's haze bore within it some ingredient that held them back. For, though they strove to penetrate it with tentacle point, those strings of unwhole-some flesh were powerless to fasten on the wreckage.

The flitter's movement toward where Simsa crouched was very slow. She could see that the whole of its bulk had cleared the opposite shore and was pointed toward the rock rim immediately below her. She had to brace her head upon her folded arm, lying near flat on the rock now, her strength seemingly continuing to drain without visible threading through the rod.

"Will!" That command was like a shout, cutting through the tangle of her thoughts and fears. "Will!"

Will the broken machine to her? Simsa of the Burrows could see little aid in that. But ruthlessly this other was taking over more and more of her mind, centering all her thought upon the wreck. *Will*—yes, let it come to her, come to her. It rang like a chant, and, though she did not know it, she was sitting up, her face frozen in a mask as she intoned aloud, though not even her own ears—only her body—knew the rhythm of that call:

"Come—come—come!"

She knew nothing of the forces that other commanded. Seemingly she was now the tool in place of the spent rod. Her hands raised from her knees, weakly wavering, but still motioning, emphasizing her chant.

"Come!"

There sounded the cry of a fighting zorsal. Simsa heard it only from a distance and as something that had no meaning now. All that did matter was that dark core of the haze moving toward this bank.

Splashing, a sucking, coughing sound. Still Simsa was not free to look, to break the compulsion holding her.

"Come!"

Something moved within the haze—something that hunched along the length of the flyer, answering to her beckoning even as the flitter appeared to do.

"Come!" One small, helpless part of her shivered, if a thought, a memory, could shiver. Did she summon one of those blob-things which had climbed to ride the wreck? In spite of that tremor within her, she waved and called for the last time:

"Come!"

The crushed nose of the wreck must be now against the rock shore below her. Once more she was herself, the power flowing out of her and leaving only a weakened husk of a person behind. The haze was fading, but that which crawled along the dark shape reached out for the rock—reached with a hand, not tentacles.

Simsa stumbled to the very lip of the rock, caught those groping hands in hers, then was herself thrown backward, another larger and hard-muscled body covering hers. She looked up into the face of Thom.

In that face the eyes were still closed. Blood trickling from his mouth spattered on her. She had strength enough to wriggle out from under his inert body, leaving him facedown and unmoving now upon the rock.

There was a sound as if some great creature had sucked or inhaled. The haze was abruptly gone. She could see the yellow horrors from the river climbing in a solid mass upon the wreckage, bearing it down the faster with their weight. Luckily they were more conscious of this invader of their own place than they were of those on the bank.

Zass cried again—a battle cry that brought Simsa's attention to where the zorsal cruised back and forth upstream. The whole surface of the sand there was pocked and heaped. There seemed no end to the creatures moving toward the wreck.

She crept forward and caught Thom by one shoulder. To turn his body over was a task almost beyond her much impaired vitality, but she managed it. Now she unsealed the uniform he wore, much as she had seen him do, in a search for injuries. Catching up the rod once again, she passed it slowly over him, hoping that through it she might learn if his hurts were critical. She thought a rib was broken, there was a contusion on his head just above the nape of his neck, and the blood, she discovered when she was able to pry his mouth open, did not come from a punctured lung as she had feared, but rather from a tear in his lower lip.

Ferwar had been, in her time, one wise enough to care for hurts such as come easily to the Burrowers. Simsa now stripped off a section of the rope she had made for crossing the other stream and tightly bound the rib. She washed the graze on his head, separating the short strands of blood-matted hair. A second piece of her rope went into the dressing of it. Last of all she dribbled a little of the water from the valley's fountain into his slack mouth, holding it shut until she felt him swallow.

When she loosed that last grip on him he stirred and muttered in a language strange to her. His eyes opened and he looked up at her, but they did not focus or show any knowledge that she was with him.

Zass flew in from the river. Now she streaked back and forth, shrieking on a note so high that Simsa's ears could barely catch it, and the girl knew that the zorsal was aroused to the peak of rage and fear.

Just as the attack of the river-thing had earlier summoned its fellows from the inland fissure, so did the uncommon commotion about the wreck, which had nearly disappeared beneath the sand, draw the others once more.

Simsa and Thom were on a small height of the rock, and the nearest fissure lay some distance away. Still the girl could see weaving yellow ribbons of unclean life streaming, jerking up into the air, across the stretch between her and that pile of

rocks which had once formed the outer point of defense of
the valley. They were cut off. Even if she could get Thom
aware, and on his feet, she could see no chance of their
escaping in that direction. And the fissures lay north and
south, as well as west, while the river was east. They were
boxed in.

There was a thing with a handgrip fastened to the belt she
had unbuckled and thrown to one side when she had searched
for the spaceman's hurts. Undoubtedly a weapon of sorts, but
how one used it and whether it would be effective against the
sand river monsters the girl had no idea.

Only they could not remain tamely where they were, to be
pulled down, torn by those deadly weaving ribbons. And she
could not carry Thom. It would seem that the Elder One had
given her this duty and then withdrawn—again, leaving her
exhausted and without resources.

There must be a uniting between the two of them. Simsa at
last accepted that, though all her normal instincts rebelled.
Back when the Elder One had first entered her, she had been
exultant, feeling whole and full of such energy and power as
she had not known could exist. Her disenchantment had
come little by little—to have one full memory and another that
was only shatters of half-seen, never understood pictures, had
been a true and growing torment. And then, when the
off-worlders had thought to take her apart as it seemed, to
shatter *her* for that broken memory, she had thought of the
Simsa of the Burrows as her shield and escape—having from
then on fought to contain those complete memories as well as
she could.

Which had sent the Elder One into hiding and brought her,

Simsa, into choices and action that was left unfinished—weak, drained, unable to fight—

Zass swooped down and settled on Thom's body, her wings fanning, her head slanted so her feather antennae were turned straight at the girl.

"Go!" That was as potent an order as her own "Come!" had earlier been.

Go she might be able to do, yes. Though at the moment she did not feel she had the strength to take more than a step or two away from this one stretch of unfissured rock. But though Thom's eyes were open and he rolled his head back and forth against her knee, crying out whenever the bandaged head wound touched the rock, he was certainly not conscious of where he was.

She leaned over him, trying to sight some knowledge of her in his open-eyed gaze. Then she thought out carefully the speech she had learned from the ship people. To speak to him in that tongue might have some effect.

"Thom Yan!" Once he had told her that that was a "friend name" used only in comradeship with those he trusted and his kin. "Thom Yan!"

The blankness of his face was troubled by a frown.

"We must go. There is trouble." She spoke slowly in the ship language, making each word as emphatic as she could. Reaching out, she drew that unknown weapon from the belt holder.

"Trouble—" She dangled the weapon before his eyes. A handgrip together with a tube. What would issue from it and how one could make it work she did not know.

Thom's lips moved. He turned his head to spit a mouthful of blood onto the rock. That small bit of action seemed to recall him to himself. Now he looked at her and his frown grew the stronger.

"Simsa—"

"Yes," she agreed. "Thom!" Now she dared take him by the shoulder and give him a small upward pull, once more holding out the weapon.

"Look!" Purposely she did not point to the riotous scene at the wreckage, but rather to those things issuing from the fissures inland—the ones that drew their slimy bodies purposefully toward their own perch.

She had steadied his head as he lifted it against her arm, and now look he did. Then his hand fell on hers and twisted the weapon out of her grip, striving to steady it as he viewed their attackers.

8

●●●●●●●●●●●●●●
●●●●●●●●●●●●●●

"Greeta! Greeta!" Thom shouted the name of the dead woman—but even that part of the flitter which contained her body was lost to view. The creatures of the sand crawled and heaped themselves most thickly on that section of the wreckage and had, by their weight, pushed it completely under, so that although here and there an end of broken metal might be seen, and the tail of the fuselage was still tilted above the surface, the rest was only a writhing struggle of the yellow things.

"She is dead," Simsa said sharply. "You cannot bring her forth from that!" She waved a hand toward the struggling mass of ovoid bodies and tangled tentacles.

Thom gave her a quick glance, and there was certainly no sign of friendliness or gratitude beneath those knotted brows or in that rage-thinned mouth. That deep anger filled him, making him forget the pain of his own hurts, Simsa sensed without being told.

He crooked his left arm at eye level, used it so to steady the barrel of his weapon. Down into that heaving mass of filthiness shot a ray of fire so brilliant Simsa closed her eyes for an instant that she might not be blinded.

Deep inside of her mind arose a scream—not from any fear or torture wreaked upon her own body, but surely coming from those sand-dwelling things now feeling the searing pain of the attack.

That faint stench which had first guided her in this direction was now a fetid cloud.

She reached up, averting her gaze from that beam, to catch his elbow with a fierce grip.

"No!" Both by word of mouth and in her mind she shouted that. "She was dead when I found you—you can do her no service, only bring those things upon us now. Would you sacrifice your life for the dead who are safely past the Star Gate and no longer aware of this world, or any other men know? She was dead! By this"—with her other hand she waved the rod before him—"will I swear it!"

For a long moment he either did not hear or else had no belief in what she said. Then that beam of deadly light was cut off, and his weapon-holding hand fell to his side, though Simsa kept her grasp on his other arm. She dragged Thom around, his back to the river, to face the long space that lay between them and that outcrop of rock which was the tricky entrance to the valley.

She had been very right to fear those fissures. Now, as she looked out over the broken surface of the plane, most of them were throwing out gouts of sand, or there were tentacles fastened on the rock that bound them at the surface, and here and there a gob of yellow was already well out of the depths and turning toward the two.

"What are they?" For the first time Thom spoke to her with a rational voice.

"Death," she returned briefly, and then added, "Here they rule. There"—she pointed to the pile of rocks which was throwing a longer and longer shadow across the plain, reaching for the very foot of the small rise on which they now stand—"there is hope—a little . . ." She was bitterly frank, for she was sure that his useless attack on the flitter's blobs had done much to arouse even the most sluggish of the crawlers. "If we can reach there. But how? Can you burn us a path, outworlder?"

He raised his weapon again to closely examine the butt of it. Simsa was able to see a thin bright red line there, as a hidden line of fire might show.

"I have half a charge still." He might have been speaking aloud to himself, for he had not looked toward her at all or made any comment on what she had said. His free hand broke out of the loose hold she had kept on him and went to a row of tubes set endwise along his belt. "Two others—that is it."

For the first time he at last regarded her.

"If we reach there"—he gestured to the distant hump of stone—"what then?"

What then indeed? She had purposely tried not to think beyond reaching the rocks. Back across the river—finding the tunnel—the valley? But the dwellers therein had already attacked Thom once—would they raise a single, jointed, hook-haired leg to aid him? This might be only a perilous interlude between two deaths. Since the Elder One had helped to raise the storm that had brought down the flitter, the valley people might be a little more merciful to Simsa. However, could she count on that? You could not guess the many turnings of the path in any alien mind. By her act in saving Thom—momentarily—she could well have condemned herself in their understanding.

Yet she had nothing else to offer but the ruined block tower—beyond the faintness of the hope that, if they could hold off the crawlers for a space, the valley people might just be moved to take a hand.

All this had passed swiftly through her mind, so she could not be sure that her words of answer did not follow directly on his question.

"I do not know—for the future"—she gave him the stark truth—"but it was once a place of protection, and I feel that these crawlers cannot venture too far from their holes." She said nothing of the valley dwellers.

She saw that he was continuing to watch her from under scowling brows.

"Was it of your raising?" he asked grimly.

Simsa did not understand. "What of what?" Had he acutely and correctly connected the storm that had downed the flitter with her fellow dweller in this body? She pressed the rod against herself and withdrew one step and then another, her attention divided between his scowling face and the weapon in his hand.

"Yes!" His scowl smoothed away, but now there was a sharp purpose in his face as his weapon swung around and up to cover her. "It *was* you!"

She retreated no farther. Confrontations back in the Burrows had taught her something of such a game, though this

was no time for the playing of games when the yellow ovoids
on the plain and their kin in the stream closed in.

"I do not know of what you accuse me." Which indeed
was no lie. She only guessed at his thoughts, would not
attempt to use the skill of the Elder One to truly read them.
"But if you wish to front me with blade and skill"—she fell
back easily into the speech and custom of the Burrows—"it
would be better to wait—we have a common enemy now."

Zass's screech nearly drowned out the last word of the
girl's speech. The zorsal dove at a yellow tip flapping along
the edge of the rock where they stood and tore at it viciously
with both tooth and talon, sending out a spurt of black-green
fluid which nearly touched Thom. Startled, he swung swiftly
to face the zorsal's opponent and aimed a beam of fire down
into the owner of that questing tentacle.

Though that finger of light was far less in its brilliance and
sweep than the power he had summoned earlier, Simsa once
again heard the dying shriek in her mind. Zass was voicing
cries of triumph, planing out from their stand toward the
interior and the rock tower as if she, also, urged on them that
way.

The nearest of the fissures had already proved a doorway
for one of the monsters. Although it swelled into greater bulk
upon coming into the air, even as they all were doing, it was
not developing such a size as either Simsa or Thom. Having
apparently made up his mind, without any further argument,
to their journey across the plain, the spaceman once more
took careful aim at that crawler. With a sharp burst of
energy, he turned it into a stinking mess of well-charred
fibers.

Simsa leapt lightly to the rock level where the creature had died, keeping well away from the mass. Its thick, sour odor seemed to cling to the air and pass from that to her skin and hair so that she gagged until she was able to control herself.

Thom had not kept up with her, and Simsa did not need Zass's warning croak to look back. The spaceman stumbled a little, one hand to his bandaged head, yet aimed his light weapon once again and took out, or at least badly wounded, another creature sliding from its fissure to cross her path. There was a humming, unlike Zass's shrieks of defiance or the sizzle-purr of the off-world weapon in use. For a breath or two of time Simsa thought the sound was coming out of the air, some form of communication between blob and blob to rally the sand creepers emerging ahead of them into an array they could not hope to blast their way through.

Thom's weapon failed. He stood, swaying a little, as he dug another cylinder from his belt loop and, shaking one such from the butt of the hand piece, forced the other in with a sharp smack. Not from him or Zass came that sound— rather it pulsated in the air weirdly as something within her stirred and answered to it.

Simsa waited for Thom to catch up. As he raised the weapon again for another shot to aim at a well-grown sand-thing, she caught at his wrist a second time. That murmur of sound was akin to the power raising of the Elder One and the yellow valley dweller.

Zass stopped in midshriek, rose higher into the air, circling about the two on the ground, the path of her circle growing farther away with every revolution the zorsal made. But it was the monsters that now surprised the girl—that and what she held in her own hand.

From the horn tips came a soft diffusion of light as unlike

the killer beams from Thom's weapon as morning mist is unlike lightning. It curled out about the two of them, enveloping them even as the wreckage in the river had been earlier hidden from Simsa's eyes. She almost expected to be caught up, taken helplessly into the air. But that whirlwind magic had been partly of the valley inhabitants—this was wholly her own.

The Elder One again—still that iron will did not move to take her over as it had so many times before. Perhaps this was only protective, preserving her from harm because of her usefulness in some future ploy. At any rate she and Thom must take advantage of it.

She crowded close to the spaceman, aware of their closeness of body that she had resented before.

"Together," she breathed, "it will hold us together—free from them—your weapon—" There was a glistening line of blue encircling the weapon's handgrip and even as she spoke he uttered a cry of pain.

"Sheathe it!" she ordered. "It is not akin to what would serve us here."

Though he had never completely lost his look of aloofness, he did slip the weapon back into the loops on his belt while the haze thickened about them. Now their clear vision reached little more than an arm's length ahead of them. Simsa thought of the fissures and wondered if their present blindness might bring them to worse than an encounter with one of the monsters. But her wonder was fleeting as she heard Zass's call from overhead. They had played this game before on night foraging when the zorsal's eyes could outsee her own. She need only to listen and Zass would guide their route for them.

At another ranging cry from Zass, without asking or seeking at all, Simsa hooked her fingers in Thom's belt and gave him a strong jerk south and forward. It would appear that he understood, for he made no resistance to her urging, though he kept his hand ready near the butt of his weapon.

They stumbled on, for Thom's weaving progress became more and more unsteady. Yet when Simsa wished to lend him her strength he muttered and thrust her away, though she did not loose her hold on his belt. There was a stain on his head bandage. When she could catch words he said over and over in a low, monotonous stream, she could understand none of them. This was not the trade-lingo of Kuxortal or the sparseness of space speech. She thought it might be his native tongue and wondered fleetingly how far he had come from the world of his birth.

Once she must have misheard Zass's warning cry, for they nearly blundered straight into a mass of waving yellow tentacles before Simsa could brace both feet against the stone to drag Thom back.

Then the haze descended once more about them like a wall and they pushed on. That curtained journey across the rock floor of this world seemed endless. Twice they stopped to rest as Zass came flitting down through the cloaking mist to perch on Simsa's shoulder and thrust her long muzzle in a moist caress against the girl's cheek.

On the second such halt the girl offered her water bottle to Thom. Although his belt had a number of pockets of small tools thrust in loops, there was no sign of any liquid carrier. Perhaps all such supplies had been in the flitter and had sunk with its dead passenger into the sand. He took several lusty swallows. Simsa had her hand raised half in protest, ready to wrestle their store away from him. But she was sure that he was only dimly conscious now, and she must keep him going on his own, for she could not handle the weight of a flaccid body should he fall. To stay here waiting for their strange cover to be penetrated by any seeking blobs was the depth of folly. Let him have the drink if it gave him the energy to keep onward.

Doggedly she kept her mind from any future—let them just reach the outpost of the valley. *Then* she could decide on the next leg of their trek.

It was getting darker and twice Thom stumbled so badly that he fell to his knees. Luckily some instinct within him kept him struggling onward, though the girl was sure he was no longer aware of her at all. Then, when it seemed that the darker haze, which was the night here, and the mist about them were so mingled together as to give them real darkness, Simsa saw a black blot of rock loom out of the curtain ahead. She loosed her hold on Thom, but she could still hear the click of his metal-soled space boots on the stone behind her as she lurched forward to fall against the sentinel rock, her breath coming in ragged sobs.

This beacon she knew, mainly because in setting forth from the ruin she had marked its fanciful resemblance to a head, the head of some grotesque creature of the never-seen, such as had been carven on the walls of that long-forgotten city on Kuxortal where the Elder One had waited so long for escape. Simsa gripped the stone with one hand. Her other fingers were so locked about the rod that they seemed numb, grown together with the force with which she held on to that weapon.

Zass's squalling cry split the gloom of this double mist as

the zorsal winged down to sit on the rock. Simsa leaned against it, spent by all her efforts. The clang-clang of the footplates did not fail. Thom came to her and oddly enough much of his wavering unsteadiness was gone. His head was a little forward, as if he fought for clarity of sight, and for the first time in what must have been half the night he spoke to her:

"Simsa?"

"Yes, it is I."

He kept on until brought up against the same rock that supported her. Now he put out a hand to touch her arm a fraction above the wrist that was cramped against the rod.

"We—we thought you—probably dead. . . ." he said slowly. "There is no shelter—and your Life Boat was deserted, the direction call half-failed. Why?"

"Why?" She rounded on him. Within her flared all the frustrations and trials that had beset her since she had made her blind landing here, bringing an anger from which she drew strength. It had always been so—that anger could burn away fear, or help her forget it a little.

"Why?" She echoed his question hoarsely. "Ask that of your friends, off-worlder. Ask it of Lieutenant Lingor, of Medic Greeta—no, she is dead. If she was a great good friend of yours . . ." That thought pricked at her. What if all of his pushing her toward those off-worlders, his stories of the Histro-Tecks—those long-lived Zacathans who would treat her as a living treasure—had been false? What if such thoughts as she had picked up from Lingor, the medic, also had dwelt in Thom's mind—that she, Simsa, was no person but a thing, as much without life or intelligence as one of the small metal images that could be dug up in the Burrows, and

sold to upper town dealers for the price of a drink or a couple of stupefying smorg leaves. What had been her price to Greeta, to Lingor—above all, to *Thom*?

As she pushed away from her rock support to face him now, the anger in her indeed giving her strength, she was all Simsa of the Burrows. The Elder One slept or was gone. Fair enough, this was her quarrel—wholly hers!

"I do not understand." There was weariness in his voice as well as in his bloodstained face. There was also stubborn determination, such as she had seen during their journeying upon her own world when he had refused to surrender his will in spite of all the obstacles that had ringed them in.

"Play not the unmind with me," she spat. "No, I have not striven to read your thoughts," she informed him as a shade of distaste seemed to come into his eyes. "Why should you think that? Were you not at ease knowing well your job was done when you betrayed me to those friends of yours! Lingor—he thought to make some plan to use what I might summon as power to make himself master among his own kind— *No!*" She gestured quickly as she saw his swollen lips open and was sure he was to dispute her words. "You need not tell me that this was not so, for that I did read in *his* mind. He was so sure of me. And she—that dead one— Greeta, who was supposed to be a healer, not a destroyer, what did she want of me? This"—she slapped her hand across her breasts—"my body! That she might cut and trace, and learn how one who was supposed to have died perhaps a million cycles of Kuxortal ages ago could walk the earth! That, too, I read past any denial. Only, I do bear her with me ever indeed—this Elder One—and by fortune her fair self, I did not ask for that burden. She summoned me, as well you know, and I could not stand before her.

"In that hour when she came into me, I felt—perhaps just what she wished me to feel to keep me to her task—that I was whole, that a part of me long severed had come back. But she is very strong and I think that she could make anyone believe as she wished. When I am threatened she awakes, and sometimes it is she and sometimes it is I, Simsa that always was, who stands to arms and awaits battle.

"She led me to read minds and then I could plan. Do you think I survived my years in the Burrows without knowing when to fight and when to run? Run it had to be from that Lingor—and your Greeta. Once that starship planeted again they could have taken me. I know so little in this life of your ways, star rover. I would have been as an unarmored dislizard is to Zass—sweet and short picking. Perhaps together those two even thought to crack my bones and get all the meat! No, the spaceport was their Burrows, they would know every turn and twist therein. Thus I made sure that they would not take me there."

"This is a dead world," he said slowly. There was not so much disbelief in him now, she thought, but of that she could not be sure.

"You are saying that this is a place of no refuge," she caught him up. But, of course, he did not know of the valley. Perhaps it was best. No, she could do nothing about that; the valley belonged to the green folk and she would take no intruder into it.

"A place of no refuge," she repeated, hoping that he had not caught the pause created by that thought. "But it is one *I* chose—one where I and any off-worlder hunting me can be equal from the start. I knew that the signal of the Life Boat might summon a ship. So Lingor turned back, did he?''

"You do not understand." He placed his weapon on top of the tall rock by which they stood. "They could not have done as you thought. There was—"

"As *they* thought," she retorted. "You delivered me up, they had me on their ship well between worlds. Yes, they were very sure of me—you were all very sure of me. Let me say this, off-worlder, it will be better to die of hunger and thirst or by blundering into the reach of one of the sand-things here than to be prisoner of those you chose to give me to!''

"I did not *choose* anything!" From the sharp note in his voice she found she had indeed pricked him then. "I am a member of the Rangers attached to the Hist-search under the orders of Hist-Techneer Zanantan. You could have stayed on Kuxortal. I asked you to come with me to meet those who have spent long lifetimes unriddling the secrets left behind— perhaps by such as your Elder One. It was for your own safety that you were given a single cabin, guarded—''

"Against your own officer, against such as Greeta?" she interrupted. "Do not speak such foolishness. The cabin— yes, it was safe enough! There were hidden places through which I could be watched, every movement of mine noted. But the Elder One could meet them trick for trick there!'' She laughed.

"Not so!" His hand formed a fist which he slammed into the rock, not seeming to notice the pain that gesture must have caused him. "You would be an honored guest. As for leaving Kuxortal, how long would you have lasted had any one of the lordlings of the upper town known the power you could wield? Speak of having your secrets out of you—they are experts at such games and far rougher than any off-worlder can guess.''

"So!" She cut him short. "The Elder One could have handled anyone coming with steel and fire. But suppose your officer, your Greeta, came to let into my 'safe place' some air to breathe which would have tied me into sleep. That was but *one* of the things they considered. Though they were not working together. No, off-worlder, I would rather take my chances on this rock than with them. The ploys of the lords I know—the crafts and slyness of your people are something else again!''

He shrugged and slipped down, his back against the rock, his hands dangling between his knees, nor had he again taken up his weapon. It was Simsa who gathered it up and tossed it to thud on the rock before him.

"We are but at the gateway of a place we may be able to defend. And the fog which protects is going.'' The cooling of the rod within her hand was a warning, and the drifting of the curtain was indeed showing thin.

He did not answer her, only pulled himself up once again, holding on to the rock. It seemed to Simsa that there was now a grayish shade to his face as though the color of the rock had somehow oozed into him even during the moments that he had been resting.

She did not wait to see if he would follow but was already in search of that way down which she had found before. Along that she climbed, the rod made fast to her girdle, using hands and toes with all the dexterity she had learned in Kuxortal. When she reached the top of the second and much taller block, the haze that had surrounded them in their journey hither had indeed threaded itself away. The sky was darker than she had ever seen it.

Calling Zass to her, she settled the zorsal on a rock point from which she could view most of the surrounding territory, including a bit of that second sand river which might offer a new threat. Simsa rolled what she had left of the cloak-made rope into a mat and settled her head upon it. The Elder One might have in her time gone without sleep to a great degree— Simsa had come to suspect that when she discovered she needed less and less rest since her body had provided shelter for the ageless one—but a body was only flesh, blood, and bone after all and also had its demands.

She was straightway plunged into a deep dark where no dreams troubled her rest. If Thom joined her on her perch, she neither knew nor cared. She no longer depended upon anyone or anything but herself and the zorsal, for Zass's single-minded loyalty had never changed, and as a camp guard the zorsal was the best.

There was the contrasting brightness of the midmorning haze when she opened her eyes again. An arm's length away lay the spaceman on his back, his eyes closed, the dried blood on his chin cracking and flaking off as he drew in long, slow breaths. Zass's cry came—faint but growing stronger as Simsa sat up and shook loose the silver lengths of her hair, combing it clumsily with her fingers. The zorsal made her usual circling descent and landed just in front of the girl. Her forepaws were tight to her body and so sheltered and protected she carried there a branch heavily laden with fruit. There was only one place the zorsal could have found that— she had been within the hidden valley. But it was what was woven around the branch that caught Simsa's attention a moment later. A tubing of some kind, transparent enough to show that it was filled near to bursting with the blue water of the pool—and that was not Zass's gift! Someone of the furred ones had wished the girl well enough to send that. Simsa gave a sigh. For the second time in her life she felt at one with something larger than herself.

The first had been when she had fronted that statue of the Elder One which had contained the essence of she who had waited and watched for so long—and now, when she could believe that those of the valley cared, even in so little!

9

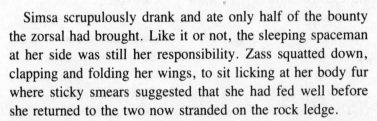

Simsa scrupulously drank and ate only half of the bounty the zorsal had brought. Like it or not, the sleeping spaceman at her side was still her responsibility. Zass squatted down, clapping and folding her wings, to sit licking at her body fur where sticky smears suggested that she had fed well before she returned to the two now stranded on the rock ledge.

Having appeased a measure of her body's need, the girl went to the edge of the block on which they had taken refuge to survey the narrow ribbon of flowing sand that lay between them and the barriers of the valley. There were no ominous writhings on its surface, nothing to suggest that there lay danger beneath that smooth roll. But she did not in the least believe that if she ventured into that murky stuff (and she had no idea as to how deep it was) she would not be in such danger as her imagination was only too willing to suggest.

Her hook and rope trick could not work again. There was

no convenient hole in the rock across the stream to catch her grapple, and she had sacrificed so much of the rope length since she had knotted it together she was sure it would not span that space. Through squinted eyes she viewed the escarpment on the other side. The haze appeared a fraction brighter, nearly as irritating to her sight as the fire in the dark tunnel had been. She dug into the memory of Simsa of the Burrows and tried to pluck forth an answer to her problem.

There was a chance—she looked to where the zorsal squatted. Zass had moved closer to the sleeping or unconscious spaceman, now and then stealthily putting forth a paw as if to touch him but quickly jerking back the limb before the gesture was complete. The zorsal apparently found the man the object of infinite curiosity—even though she had once traveled for days in his company on Kuxortal.

Simsa turned to face the plain over which they had come. Though none of those ominous lumpings of sand were being spit forth from the fissures, and no yellow tentacles had thrust up into sight, she knew that to set foot again on that surface was to offer a challenge to the sand dwellers.

The Elder One— She shook her head violently. No. She would open no doors, would have no part in lending her body to the other's superior wisdom! No appeal to the Elder One. *She* was the Simsa of the here and now, and as such she would solve—

Her thoughts were broken by a hacking cough. The eyes of the man were open, and he had lifted himself up to lean on one elbow and regard her.

After one measuring glance his gaze shifted to the rocks about them, the heights beyond the sand stream. The tip of his tongue crossed cracked lips. Simsa moved, bringing to him half of Zass's bounty which she had spared in spite of her own thirst and hunger. Thom sat up, squeezing first a portion of the water into his mouth.

"Where does this come from?" He weighed the still not empty tube in his hand. Perhaps it was the needs of his body that made his voice so harsh.

Simsa could see nothing to be gained now in keeping the valley oasis a secret. Without his flitter Thom could not return to any of his own kind who might be encamped where she had brought down the Life Boat. Nor did she undervalue the dwellers within and their powers. They had already brought an end to one invader of their world and could hold them both at their pleasure.

"There." She pointed to the rock wall that raised such a formidable barrier against them. "There is water, fruit—a place of growing things."

"There is also more, is there not?" he returned, breaking one of the blue fruit apart, licking the pulp from his grimed and stone-bruised hands. "That whirlwind which struck a little too quickly and accurately. Your people—your home world?" He gestured with sticky fingers at what lay about.

"No!"

"But one you know well enough to be not only able to survive but to protect yourself against any dangerous surprise."

She was not aware that she had once more pressed the crescent-crowned rod between her breasts until there was a feeling of small warmth in it. She glanced down and saw the points of light, like two gleaming Caperian sapphires, glistening where there was no sun to draw such an answer.

She did not know this world. But—did the Elder One? At least that inward dweller had matched the power of the furred one quickly enough. They might have been old partners in such a defense, or weapon.

"I do not know this world." She held her voice steady; in at least half she was speaking the truth. "You are a star traveler—I am not. I cannot read the star maps. And Life Boats choose the nearest world which has breathable air for those seeking escape—so your own instructions to voyagers read. If this was the nearest world on which we could breathe . . . then that was it. I did not pilot the Life Boat. Who can?"

"Still there is other life here besides those monsters of the sand."

He chewed the last of the fruit skin and swallowed it. Then he picked up the water-bearing tube and swung it slowly back and forth as if intending by this gesture to refute any easy lie that might occur to her. "Your zorsal did not fill this—that I will not believe—no matter how well the creature has been trained."

"You do not truly train a zorsal!" she snapped, playing for time before she made that other answer which she must truly give. "Yes, that was filled—by others—another. But I know no more of this world than that others *do* abide. And they are not humanoid, though they appeared to me well intentioned."

To her, perhaps, but she did not forget the raising of the whirlwind—nor, apparently, did he, for he gave a harsh sound that might have been laughter, except there was no lighting of that in his expression.

"They are well intentioned?" Thom made both a question and an accusation out of those four words.

"To me—to Zass—welcome was given."

"But not to any scouring their skies—is that it?" He had lifted himself as far as his knees. Now with effort, Simsa making no move to aid him, he got to his feet and crossed to her side where he might look down at that sinister, half-solid flood circling there.

"How did you cross before?" he wanted to know, having stood a long moment in silence.

Tell him of the light path of belief— No! But the grapple anyone knowing of the Burrows would well accept as natural. She explained what she had done and that it could not serve them now, because of the lack of torn-fabric rope and the fact that there was no anchor on the other bank.

Thom did not even answer her. Instead he leaned well out, back once again on his knees, looking along that section of this heap of stone which fronted on the river.

"If I knew how deep . . ." He might have been voicing some thought aloud. Now he slipped from its loop on his belt the ray weapon he had used in their flight. Knocking the small charge from the butt into his hand, he examined it closely.

"To set foot on that—" Simsa did not know what he intended, but she was sure that anything venturing on the sand stream would sink beyond aid, even if he or she was not attacked instantly by the dwellers therein. But Thom was not peering downward. Rather, he turned his head to the left to inspect the edge of the platform on which they now perched. The new vigor of his movements revealed he must have made up his mind about something as he got to his feet. He spoke with the old authority she remembered well from the days of their first meeting on Kuxortal.

"If that rock—the one with the three lumps along it—is

undercut, it will fall forward. Two more cuts there and there"—he used the barrel of his weapon as a pointer—"ought to bring down a rockslide. Let that reach this river and we may well have a dam over the top of which we can pass—if we are fast enough."

"You can do this with your weapon?"

He nodded but was frowning. "I believe so, but it will also near exhaust this charge, and if we meet with trouble beyond . . ." He shrugged.

He was not fashioned to show much patience in the face of danger. Simsa had sensed that from the hour of their first meeting. Neither was she. But the path on the other side of that flood was a rough and narrow one, twice forcing her farther away from the proposed crossing to cling like a nix-beetle to the stone and edge along. If the inhabitants of the stream were aroused, a mere crossing of their dwelling place was not going to bring much safety. On the other hand, to remain spinelessly where they now perched would achieve nothing either.

Simsa turned the rod around in her hands, rolling it back and forth between her palms. Might this weapon-tool of the Elder One serve also? Best not try, she decided swiftly. She needed all her native wits about her; she had no idea of turning any part of their escape over to that indweller. It might well be that the Elder One had no wish to get Thom free of the valley or even continue to allow him life.

Her own attitude toward the off-worlder had made such a number of subtle changes lately that she could not be sure she would be able to rise and combat the Elder One on that point. So she remained silent, offering no assistance.

He was very careful in the aiming of his weapon, several

times lying belly down upon the rock and then getting up to move again when the proposed angle of the beam seemed not to his liking. But at length he fired.

The ray that shot from the barrel was wider than before, and there was also a puff of acrid smoke which set her eyes to watering and made Zass squawk indignantly and take to flight. Nor did the zorsal return; rather, she winged out and up toward the rim of the hidden valley.

However, the fire sprayed across the lumped rock that was Thom's choice for undercutting, the stone disappearing as if it had never had existence. The block fell forward. To Simsa's astonishment, for she had not really believed in Thom's promise, two other huge stones followed, crashing into the first and driving it on into the river.

There was a dam almost before she could draw a deep breath again. The first rock had disappeared, eaten up by the swirling grit, but the second which had followed kept its upper surface above the rising sand.

Thom returned his weapon to its loop with one hand, the other one caught tight about her wrist.

"Jump! Jump!"

She could do no else than follow his command, for he had already moved to leap and would not release his hold. Thus they threw themselves forward together, he loosing his hand only as they left their rock of refuge. Simsa fell as she had been trained, adding new bruises to her score.

Thom was already up, once more reaching for her. The sand was banking higher, rivulets forced their way across the lower edge of the topmost block. There was no time to hesitate. She sprang first, reaching a higher landing on the other side, swinging around to narrowly watch the sand.

That pocking and lumping which had been the signal for the monsters' attack before was beginning again. Simsa brought out the rod. It might well be all that was between them and death now—if, as he feared, his weapon was exhausted.

Just beyond was a narrow strip of small stone-marked beach. Where they had landed were rocks and already Thom had his back to those, was glancing from the weapon he had drawn again to those movements of the sand about the improvised dam.

Simsa looked up hopefully. There were no promising hollows here. The cliff wall was sheer above a level with her head. Zass, who had returned to circle over them on that wild venture across the fallen rocks, gave a series of guttural cries and rose higher in ever-widening circles, one of which finally reached beyond the edge of the cliff. She did not return. The girl felt the warmth of the rod and knew that if they must make a stand, this fight was again hers as well as his. Could the haze that had been before summoned once more give them cover?

Deep in her there was a stir. The Elder One was rousing, and, seeing a tentacle stretch from the river toward her, Simsa knew that this time perhaps a surrender on her part to that other personality might be their only chance at safety.

"Can you cover me?" Her companion's demand was sharp, and Simsa, concerned with her own apprehension at the stirring of the Elder One, looked at him in confusion.

He was wrestling with his weapon, turning its butt around in his hand, tapping it against his palm.

"With that thing of yours"—he was even more impatient now—"can you hold them back for a space?" He nodded at the rod.

"What do you plan?" she asked, then swung the rod around so that the ray shot from the tip of the nearest moon crescent to transfix a yellow sucker-marked pointed ribbon, as thick as Thom's wrist, which flailed at the spaceman's scuffed and battered boots.

"We need stairs. Hold them and I shall see what can be done!"

Almost mechanically and without aim she swept the glow of the rod across the now fiercely troubled sand surface. Thom wheeled about to face that expanse of sheer rock. Did he think to bring down another rockslide? But what would that profit him if they were buried in it?

What shot from the barrel of his weapon was not the wide beam that had eaten out the rocks and reduced the monster company to odorous ash as they crossed the plain. Instead, a ray no thicker than her smallest finger was aimed steadily while a blackened hole appeared. Another and another, each some distance apart. Yes—a ladder which would not give under their strength but instead afford them a way out!

Reassured that Thom knew what he was doing, Simsa kept to her own task, that of driving the sand creatures off. Perhaps they had learned the threat of the rod from her earlier attacks upon their kind, for they were in no hurry to crawl out of their holes. Tentacles waved and were reduced to oily smears. Then, though the sand heaved and whirled in an even more frenzied manner, there came no more signs of creatures emerging.

A muffled exclamation brought her head around for an instant or two. Simsa could see that the ray from his weapon, thin and light as it was, had begun to ripple along its length, and she guessed that the source of its energy was failing.

Thom flitted it more quickly now from the carving of one space to the gouging out of the next, racing against both time and his dwindling resource. The last dark splotch before the ray utterly disappeared was hardly more than a very shallow groove. Tucking the now useless weapon-tool back in his belt, Thom knelt to jerk at the latches on his space boots, freeing his feet and locking the footgear by their fastening to his belt.

He gave a last glance to the boiling surface of the stream and then jerked a thumb at the cliff fast.

"Climb!"

Simsa resolutely shook her head. "Go yourself. I will stay and buy us what time fortune will favor."

Thom stared sharply at her and then centered his gaze on the rod, almost as if he would will that into his own hand as he had made the rocks earlier do his bidding. But it was plain without any more words between them that this game must be played by her rules and not his.

He turned and caught at the first of the holes he had cut in the barrier while Simsa, drawing upon all the depths of will within her, allowed the Elder One to venture forth.

Ah, this space-going intelligence was apt in a point of peril. Yes, one must well keep one's eyes upon such species, for they learned so quickly that they often neglected the proper controls in their search for raw power. However, this was no time to argue the points of any such case. Simsa, the Elder One, flourished the rod as she would a whip to send some shadow lurker squalling. The bluish ray became a cloud to thicken and slide across the sand.

Thom made good time up the rock ladder, and Simsa, tucking the rod to safety, followed. But as she climbed she discovered that the failure of the weapon he had used was marked by the shallow indentation of the high holes. She did not look down or try to squint upward at the other climber. Instead she slowed until a voice from above brought her to a stop.

"Not so fast—these are the hardest—" Thom called hoarsely, as if the effort he had forced his body to was sapping once more his small measure of strength.

How long did he believe she could continue to hang there by her fingers and toes? This was proving a far harder journey, even with no darkness and no pit of flames, than the first she had taken into the lost valley.

She could hear a scrambling sound, the hard breathing of one putting his body to an ultimate task. So much did Simsa of the Burrows hear, but the interpretation came from the Elder One.

This new race of space-faring species had determination, even if their unopened minds hampered them so much. Tools were things outside themselves, dead things of wood and metal, until they were roused to limited life. It seemed clearer and clearer that they were unaware, totally unaware, of other potentialities. What could they not accomplish if they learned—

And how would lives across the star lanes be changed if they did? For good or ill? Those two on the ship who had thought to use her—*her*—for their own knowledge, were there an overnumber of such among these new people?

The Elder One speculated and her thoughts passed through Simsa's mind, hinting that perhaps, when there was time and space for privacy, she might be set a number of difficult questions by this other self of hers. For the moment that strength which filled the Elder One kept her as tight and safe against the stark wall as if she stood on a well-balanced ledge. She did not fear that her grip with fingers and toes might be lost.

More scrambling sounds from above and then something dangled down the cliff face to nearly strike her in the face. The belt of the spaceman, its loops stripped of all the tools and weapons that he might carry, swung close to her left hand, and she dared to loosen her hold to seize upon it.

But she did not rest her full weight upon that tie; rather, she still climbed, with the belt wreathed tightly around her arm as a support. Then a hand reached down, laced fingers into the jeweled belt that held her kilt, and heaved her up and over the lip of stone, grazing her flesh in the process in a rough end to that journey. Once more they had found refuge on a flat level of rock—one so wide she had begun to think that they had lost the valley descent that lay to the north and that this was merely more of the plain raised to a greater height.

The sky haze was thick, seeming to curdle about the two of them as though it were a serpent winding its length back and forth across the sky, now nearly touching the rock at their feet, now capriciously raising to give them great range of sight.

Simsa saw Thom sitting only a little away from the cliff edge, his belt in a coil about his feet, his bandaged head and arms limply forward as though he had spent the last of that burst of strength which had brought him this far.

She scrambled up to stand gazing north and west. Somewhere there cut the valley with all its promise of food, drink, and shelter—or perhaps its threat from the furred ones who had already brought down the invading flitter. They had welcomed her after a fashion, but how would they greet Thom or treat her for bringing him hither? Simsa of the Burrows arose in her to demand that from the Elder One. But the latter was still in command of her slender dark body and was turning her a fraction to face what seemed a deepening of the haze.

The penetrating cry of Zass broke the silence of the cliff top as the zorsal planed down to Simsa's shoulder, nuzzling against her cheek with soft chirrups. Then, through that heavier gathering of the haze, came moving shapes. The girl braced herself. Perhaps none of the blob-things could climb this high, but it was plain that someone—or something—had come seeking them.

10

The first of the half-seen shapes emerged from the mist, one of the green furred people of the valley. Simsa half expected to sight a weapon in those claws of the upper appendages. Or was this creature only war-armed with such mysteries as the Elder One had helped them to call up? There was no way of reading either anger or suspicion on a face that was mainly huge eyes and a mandible-equipped mouth.

Thom fought to his feet, wavering there as he stood to confront the newcomers. On impulse the girl moved closer to him, not to help but because she intended to knock from his hold any weapon he might produce for attack. But both hands dangled at his sides. He seemed to be expending the full amount of any energy left him just to hold up his head in order to face these newcomers squarely.

For more than one of the valley dwellers followed in the wake of the first, moving out to form a half circle, all facing the two humans and Zass. Simsa had seen enough tapes, enough strangers from off-world in flesh, fur, or scales, not to be surprised at the strange forms into which nature had fitted intelligence on other worlds. Somehow she was sure that Thom would realize that now they dealt with "people" and not with monsters intent only on the hunt.

But it was the Elder One who was still in charge, and Simsa found herself mouthing strange syllables which she could not translate but which she knew were a mingled greeting and plea for understanding. Judging by the only standards she understood—those of the Burrows—she was content to let this other carry the argument.

Having uttered that strange hum-hiss of speech, she remained where she was, the rod now held up before her, as a runner on her home world, sent to clear the road, might carry the House-crest of a lordling as he sped ahead of that lord's entourage. She felt the combined sight of those others. How she could sense such impact she could not explain. It was almost as if the dead Greeta had, in a manner, achieved her desire, and all the parts that went to make up Simsa's black, silver-haired body had been laid open to be observed, weighed, disputed over—or accepted.

The leader of the valley force went to all fours to approach closer, the clack-clack of those long claws sounding louder. Simsa looked to Thom. The man had somehow conquered the weakness he had before shown and stood with straight shoulders and upheld head. His hands moved in a very ancient gesture of peace which was common enough to the species she did have knowledge of. Both his hands were held on a level with his shoulders, his bare palms exposed to the strangers' sight. He wanted no struggle.

"This—one—from—overhead?"

The question was awkwardly phrased, but Simsa understood. "Yes."

"From—this—you—ran?"

"Not this one." Simsa was willing to give Thom the benefit of the doubt. After all, he had never held such thoughts concerning her future as those other two revealed.

"Why—here?"

"For me"—she could not evade that—"but he is not an enemy."

Was she right in declaring that? Even now she could not be sure.

"What does he, then?"

"He is a hunter of old knowledge. He believes I have such knowledge—he would take me to those who gather it."

"He is—not—of—the—home. He is of the short-lived kind."

If thoughts could hold contempt, that fairly dripped from the speech she caught with the Elder One's aid.

"He—not as those you know." A flash of knowledge came to her then, such as so often broke through the barriers set by Simsa of the Burrows' wary mind. These creatures were female—or at least of a sex approaching what her own kind thought female. They equated Thom with a state of being to which they had long ago reduced their own male counterparts—a small but necessary evil. Certainly very short-lived, if they had their own way in the matter.

"He is a hunter of knowledge," she continued sharply. The shadow thought of what was expedient to do with mere males had come too fast upon the uttering of the judgment of his usefulness.

"Paugh!" An exclamation of disgust was not easily translated to words but came from the spokeswoman of that other party. "What has such as he to store knowledge in?"

On impulse Simsa spoke aloud to her companion. "They—I do not know how much you may have picked up from thought reading—but these hold males in contempt. Will you open your mind to them—and quickly."

She was not even sure that the spaceman could "think" a message plainly enough. Her own hold on such powers was shaky and she was only sure of success when the Elder One was in control.

There flashed speedily a series of pictures, aimed surely for the furred doubter or doubters but as easily picked up by the girl.

It was like watching one of the reading tapes run a little too fast to be enjoyed but showing so many changes and hints of knowledge as made her feel breathless. Then she saw the leader of the valley ones squat back on her lower abdomen, balanced by the two long folded legs. She swung up a clawed forelimb, the murderous claws held well apart, perhaps her own type of peace signal.

"A Memory one!" There was an exclamation of wonder in that mind speech. "A Memory one, be it male or not. Tshalft must suck this one for herself."

"No!" Simsa took a wide sidestep which put her between the valley dwellers and Thom. There was a connotation to that word "suck"—or so it had sounded to her—that carried a dark meaning.

"No harm to it," came the quick promise. "It has too much to give. We try—our Memory ones are few—and there come many hatchings before one is discovered in these days.

To have new knowledge, that will be treasure for the home. We shall do it no harm, even as we have done none to you. But will it be hunted again? Has it laid some trail for its kind to follow?''

"Will you—" began the girl, when he spoke swiftly, proving that he had read that mind speech.

"The flitter is down. But there are others on the ship which landed here. When they cannot raise any call from us they may write us off—for now.''

"But not forever?" Simsa prodded.

"Zasfern is not easily thrown off the trail of anything which is as great as the discovery of a true Forerunner," he answered her. "They may not be able to search now, but in time they will come, yes. My immediate superior, Hist-tech Zasfern, has power with the service.''

"It speaks of others," came the thoughts of the valley leader. "Who are these others?''

Thom raised his hand and pushed fretfully at the bandage about his head. "Answer for me," he said to the girl. "Ask them not to mind read me now—I—" He stumbled half-toward her. Unthinkingly she took his weight, which bore her with him to the stone.

Over his body she looked up at the others. "He is hurt.''

"That is so," conceded their seated leader. "Now his thoughts go all ways, as the guden fly when it is time for a harvest. What would he have you tell us?''

"I know little more than you. But he has said there is a very ancient race whose mission it is to collect all knowledge and store it. They are very old, but it is true that most they gather is from such a long time in the past that they do not understand much of it themselves. They only hunt and hunt for scraps to be fitted into a whole. They have said that is why I must be brought to them. For they think that I—she—can match some of these scraps for them.''

"So they will be led to seek here. When?"

"Sometime hence I think." Simsa shifted Thom's head upon her knee. He gave a small moan and rolled his face toward her so that she felt the light flutter of his breath against her skin. "He must have help." She found herself adding that plea.

"It is well—for now. Yes, we have much to learn—Tshalft would wish us to do this."

A click of claws summoned one of the others. With no visible sign of any discomfort because of his weight, the speaker plucked Thom out of Simsa's half hold and placed him on the back of the follower squatting before her. One of those claws grasped both of the dangling arms of the spaceman, imprisoning his wrists in a single hold. Then the creature turned and started away three-legged but seemingly not in the least slowed or disturbed by that. Simsa and the speaker followed.

This time there was no journey into the dark, but the top of the barrier was wide and they were soon near curtained from each other's sight by a thickening of the haze. Simsa found her own wrist caught in the claws of another, steering and drawing her onward when the haze at last thickened into a roof too dense for the eye to pierce beyond a foot or so.

They came to the top of a stairway and the grasp on Simsa fell away—only the one pointing claw directed her downward. The steps were stone, chiseled out of the rock. For her feet they were narrow, and, since so much was hidden from her, she took them one at a time, her right hand braced against the side wall, her fingers ready to cling to any projection they might chance upon.

She had lost all sight of Thom and his guardian and tried to force out of her mind a suggestion of danger—a fall for the awkwardly laden valley inhabitant and perhaps the end of the unconscious man as a result.

Down and down wove the stairs—there were no landings where one might pause to get one's breath, summon up courage for further effort, and the fog was as tight as a cloak about them. Then that began to thin and wisps of it moved away as clouds could be driven across the sky by the wind—only here there was no wind.

She could see the way ahead for a much farther space now. But there was nothing but more and more steps. Simsa might well have given out long ago, but that extra energy which the Elder One always brought with her sustained the girl even when the presence of the Elder One herself began to slowly retreat into that part of Simsa which she had established as her own abode for all time.

The last of the haze was tattered strips. Here and there she could sight a tall standing tree of high-growing vegetation, much like those that had formed the avenue at her first coming to this place. The zorsal uttered a small cry and took off, winging ahead, apparently diving into the massed vegetation which Simsa would have thought was far too thick to allow any wing spread. They reached at last the floor of the inner valley. She could smell the heady scent of dropping fruit and she licked her lips, the odor immediately bringing with it hunger.

There was a path here, not as well marked as those she had

found earlier, and it did not stretch straight forward but wound around among bushes that were taller than the girl's head. Palm-wide flowers clustered thick over these, weighting those toward earth where crawled a number of green winged things which in a minute way were not too unlike her guides. Among the bushes some of the furred people were moving. These claws which could threaten so menacingly worked here with delicate care, loosing one after another of the busy feeding insects, holding them above jugs until, from the tip of rounded green abdomens, a drop of clear liquid gathered to drip into the waiting container. Its donor was then returned to the grazing ground of the flowers.

At the appearance of the party from the cliffs these harvesters drew together and stared silently, nor did Simsa pick up any thought save once or twice a feeling of dislike or alien aversion radiating from them, something she had not felt before. It would seem that her presence, or Thom's, or both, was a matter for resentment.

Yet there were no claws raised even a fraction, and their own party plowed ahead through the wandering trails of the flowered-bush land without any communication she could sense. In a few strides they left the workers behind.

This was a wider way they had now turned into. Ahead, though still some distance away, the girl caught sight of that odd dwelling or fortress she had seen before. However, they were not headed for that. A side way opened in the brush and into it stalked the furred one carrying Thom, then the leader of the company, raising a claw to beckon Simsa to follow. The others kept on in the open and were quickly lost to sight as this side way made a right-angled turn. It would appear, Simsa thought, that they were heading back toward the cliffs

down which they had just come. But when they emerged
from the growth that was so thick a screen here, there was
again a wide space as there had been about the fountain.

No spray of water spun into the air here; rather, the open
place, a triangle, cradled what Simsa first thought was a giant
egg. At least it presented a solid-looking ovoid to the newcomers. Their party halted just at the verge of the open space
and the leader advanced, not with that measure of authorita-
tive stride-hop which she had shown earlier, but slowly,
using the claws of a right fore appendage to tap out a rhythm
on the bare ground.

Though the tapping was so small a sound that Simsa could
barely hear it, there was an answering in the ground itself
which ran along the surface of the earth, even into her own
body so she found herself moving with the same beat, her rod
nodding in turn in her hold.

It appeared that whatever or whomever the leader so summoned was not minded to answer. Yet the tapping continued
patiently. There came at last a sharp pop. Across the surface
of that giant egg appeared a ragged crack. A portion of shell
detached, to fall upon the earth. Then a second and a third,
until the shell was in fragments. They were fronting now
another of the furred ones. In size she was smaller; she had
been cramped and fitted into the egg without much room to
spare so that when a forelimb moved slowly into the open it
did so feebly, as though any effort were nearly too much for
the slowly arousing creature within.

There was a sleekness, as though it had been immersed in
water that now dripped and runneled to the ground. Then the
faceted eyes which Simsa had thought were blind centered
upon them.

"Why—come—disturb?"

There was anger bordering on rage in that demand from the egg prisoner.

"A Memory one—from far—sky." The leader braced both forelimbs on the ground and lowered her own antennae-feathered head so that those lacy sheaths nearly brushed the pounded earth.

The other had managed to pry her body free. With her last jerk what remained of the shell crumbled into powder on the ground. She made a slight gesture with one set of claws and the leader hastened, still on all fours, to approach near, pausing at a small distance which Simsa read as one of respect, to unhook a smaller edition of the harvester jugs from a belt and offer it to the newly hatched. Greedily the other seized upon it and drank until at last she turned it upside down to prove its emptiness.

She moved alertly now and Simsa was able to note the differences between her and those other of the valley dwellers the girl had seen. The head was certainly out of proportion, larger, and the fur was lighter, banded with a very faint darker striping.

"It—was—not—time," the egg born announced. "To disturb is forbidden—only a matter of great importance—"

The leader echoed that last expression. "Great importance!" She must be slightly servile to this other, but she was standing her ground about what she had done.

Simsa was aware of the huge eyes (they looked even larger than the others of this race she had yet seen) turned on her. Movement beside her came as the bearer of Thom released her burden to sprawl on his side. But it was Simsa that the strange one first surveyed. And it was the Elder One who

moved forward to receive that searching, inimical stare, eye
to faceted eye, until the egg born said:

"This one—in the time of the lost moon—this one—"

"Not so," the Elder One answered at once. "My blood kin,
perhaps—not me. I am new into the world as the Most
Strong Memory herself."

"Too much—too long—then the egg again," the other
thought. "If not you then—why you now?"

"New come from egg, I seek my people."

"Did they not guard—wait—know the signal rightly?"
There was a note of indignation in that. "There must always
be those who know—who can call."

Simsa the Elder One shook her head. "Too long—too
long. Those who might have watched went I know not
where."

"Yet you stand here? What loosed you, then?"

"The coming of one reborn, of my kin reborn—she I
summoned—but I had no body. My egg did not hold me, so
thus I am in her."

"Ill done. Seek you a body, eggless one?"

"This one serves me well—it is kin born and so mine. We
walk the same path and all is well."

"What seek you here?" The fur of the other was rapidly
drying and the darkened stripes were more sharply defined. It
put out one forearm to its head as if to support that still too
large cranium.

"Safety—for a space," Simsa returned promptly.

"This other—" The large eyes for the first time regarded
Thom. "Is he dying? Have you already quickened and used
him and now await your own body eggs? If that be so, why

bring him hither? Let his body return to the earth since he is of no further use.''

"He is not my seeder of egg life.'' The Elder One seemed to know exactly the right answers. "He is a Memory Keeper.''

If a furred, facet-eyed creature could look affronted and disgusted, Simsa believed that this one did.

"He is male—they are good for only one thing. There has never been a Memory one among them—never!'' There was angry indignation in that.

"Probe and see, Great Memory Keeper, probe you, and see.''

Simsa found herself moving slightly away from the prone spaceman as if to clear a wider path for the other's thoughts. On the ground Thom stirred and made a querulous sound.

The girl had an impression of a thought stream almost as visible as an outpouring of fluid, and the greedy sucking up of the same. Yet the Elder One did not share what was happening.

Simsa could set no length to the time that exchange continued. Again Thom raised a hand to his head as if to protect himself from some blow. He muttered unceasingly. Simsa picked up words of the trade-lingo, but she was sure that he also spoke in several different tongues during that weird communication—if communication might be the term to apply to this one-sided interrogation. Then he was at last still and the big eyes lifted from his face to rivet their full attention on the girl.

"It is true! Memory cannot be kept hidden from a rememberer—or, it is said, in any way altered more than the alteration which occurs from the event's action appearing thus to one, otherwise to another. These Zacathans—these who seek memories, not to keep them in trained minds but in other ways—he is of importance to them?''

"Judge that for yourself from what you have gained from this man. He served them as the tenders serve you, bringing bits and pieces he has learned for their combined memory.''

"But they have no true memory—no true rememberer.'' Again that feeling of hostility.

"Each to their own, Memory one. If knowledge be kept, what matters the exact way of its keeping?''

The other raised both claws to her oversized head. "I have a this-way, that-way in my head, egg born. Too much, too fast, and I not yet ready to break shell when it was loosed upon me! Let this one be kept—and tended—and you—be welcome among us. But we are the apart ones and if any more strangers come seeking, let them hunt out on the plain. For we shall set up the barriers. Much—much to think on—to sort out. Much!''

She seemed to crumple, to draw in upon herself, squatting down among the remnants of the egg. Now the one who had borne Thom here picked him up with the leader's aid and turned abruptly, even as two of her kind came bursting into the clearing. They pushed aside Simsa and the leader to close upon the Great Memory, stroking her fur, holding forth another jug, a much larger one, for her to drink from, while those with Simsa and Thom urged retreat.

They were not to be quartered in the tower that served as a residence for most of the valley, Simsa discovered; rather, they were taken along the cliff side to where there was a cave that gave a measure of shelter. Long plant leaves were brought in bundles by the furred ones and then were speedily teased into two beds. Food appeared in the form of fruits spread out on another large stiff leaf, and Zass found her way to them just as Thom roused. The furred ones were gone so that they were alone.

He levered himself up on one elbow with a groan and looked around him, plainly puzzled. "Where is this?" he asked in trade-lingo. "And where is Zasfern—he was waiting for my report. I do not understand. I was in the foreroom of the ministry and Zasfern was asking questions. It seemed as if he asked hundreds of them—all about our past surveys. Why—"

The spaceman might have been talking to himself. Now he saw her. At that same moment the Elder One also loosed her grip and it was the Simsa he had first known who faced him.

"Where is this place?" There was more force and spirit in his demand. "I take it I was not with Zasfern, so who turned my mind inside out?" He rubbed the palms of both hands across his forehead as if seeking to erase pain.

"It was the Great Memory," Simsa began her answer, not sure he would believe her, and related all that had happened from the moment they had met the furred ones on the cliff top to the present.

"A memory trained to hold all knowledge—" Thom repeated when she had done. "I would have sworn that was impossible. But perhaps on this forsaken world there have been so few happenings of importance that it could be done. If you saw the great banks of computers in Zath City . . ." He shook his head and winced. "That is now the memory for most of the known worlds, and it would take a thousand Zacathans a good thousand of their life years to begin to shift it all. No one could hold that. But this Great Memory does believe I can here gather knowledge rather than harm her people?"

"You came here for me," Simsa responded tightly. "That I have not forgotten even if you suddenly choose to do so."

11

· · · · · · · · · · · · · ·
· · · · · · · · · · · · · ·

Here in the valley the thickening of haze marking the nighttime was stronger. Simsa, sitting at the mouth of the cave, gazed out over the expanse of brush and trees where shadows appeared to gather and wrap around each living thing. From behind her came the low, even rhythmic breathing of Thom's sleep. His ordeal of mind search at the hands—or thoughts—of the Great Memory had undermined his strength more than he would admit, and he had slept away most of the rest of the day since they had been left at this refuge.

There had been no guards set to see that they stayed where they were. Still, Simsa did not doubt that, if she descended that slope into the cover of vegetation, she would not move without eyes upon her. There might be a very thin line between captive and guest.

Zass, wings furled, was curled next to the girl, the greater heat of the zorsal's body warm against her flesh. For the moment she was alone again—the Elder One was gone from the forepart of her mind. She was thinking fiercely, making one plan and discarding it as quickly while she sat there motionless.

Food and water, all her body might need for existence, were here. But she had begun to understand that it was entirely possible she was as firmly a prisoner here as she had been in the ship. Only—Simsa smiled crookedly—*then* she had had her own plans. The difficulty that now lay before her was that her plan had succeeded. She was free of the ship, from the designs the officer and Greeta had nursed in their minds. But if her future freedom was to be encased in this valley, of what benefit was it to her? No, she had been too quick to move when she had stolen the Life Boat and come here. She should have waited until she was closer to the well-traveled star lanes where planets able to support life would have been more abundant.

Between her idle hands the rod twirled. It was without light now, just an unusual artifact of a race long since disappeared. It would seem that in her way she, too, was such an artifact. Perhaps even a possession to be fought for. Where did she go now—what must she do?

That she would meekly go to ground here . . . no, that was not for her. Though Simsa sat statue still, restlessness fired within her. Surely there was a way out! She refused to believe that this early in her wanderings she had been brought to a firm stop.

"No moon—"

Those words out of the dusk of the cave at her back startled her. It was easy to forget Thom's presence for long moments at a time.

"Why did you come?" she demanded abruptly, not mind to mind but in trader tongue.

"You were—are—here."

"And what is that to you, spaceman?" She was glad she could get such a hard note into her voice. "How well were you paid to bring me to those? Or had they not yet paid and you would not lose your prize?"

"I cannot believe—"

Simsa did not turn to look at him, rather dug the point of the rod into the grayish earth. "Do not, then. I know what that officer, that woman of your breed, would have of me. And who knows what else their superiors might plan. If I could tear out of me now that other one, I would give her to you—or sell her." Again Simsa grimaced. "I am of the Burrowers and one sells, one does not give. Yes, I would sell her to you readily enough. When she first came to me . . ." She returned in thought to that moment in the strange temple where she had found her double frozen in time, undoubtedly worshipped by the forgotten race who had succeeded her own. "Yes." She spoke more swiftly. "When she came to me I felt—whole—greater—alive. Until I knew that for her I was only a body, by some chance of strange fate a body born later in time and yet of her people, by resemblance. Then . . ." She bowed her head a little, trying in her own mind to sort out what she had felt then, that the Simsa she knew was a nothing, a spark that could be easily extinguished by this great fire. Yet stubbornly she had risen to the challenge, to fight, to remain at least in part what she had always been.

"Was it not better"—his voice had the old calm she had known during their first journey together—"to become the greater—rather than the lesser?"

Simsa's mouth worked, she spat defiantly, even though he
might not see the whole of that gesture of repudiation since
her back was to him.

"Speak not of alms until you wear the beggar's sores,"
she repeated an old saying. "I know only that at times I am
one thing and at some instances I am another." She turned
her upper body a little to one side so she could see him where
he lay stretched on one of the bed bundles, his arms folded
under his head to raise it a little.

"She—I—brought down that flitter of yours! She—I—joined
in with these of the valley and caused one death of your
people and meant no less for you. Do you still speak for
her?"

"Yet you came to find me, and else that had not passed, I
would have died. Why save me?"

"Perhaps she had a reason."

"Not you, then, but this other?"

Somehow he was forcing the truth out of her. "Have it
your way, star rover. Yes, I came for you. There was too
much in the past that I would see you dead without a chance
of defense. We walked strange trails together once."

"Just so. And now we would walk others, it would seem.
They will be searching for the flitter, you know. I do not
know how good the sand river is at burying what it takes, but
the flitter recorder will continue to send messages for a
space—a beacon."

She pounded one knee with her fist. "Your lieutenant must
be very sure of what he wants."

"What did you discover which made you do this thing?"
He hoisted himself slowly to a sitting position. "You said

that that officer wanted you for what profit he might make, that Greeta wanted you to—"

"To cut flesh from bone and see why I am what I am, yes! I told you they set me apart in a cabin with hidden peepholes that they might watch me, perhaps test me in some way. She—the Elder One—found those with no trouble at all and made for them covers—hallucinations. Tell me the truth, spaceman—if you had gotten me to these Zacathans of yours, would they have done any better?"

"They do not work in that way."

"Ha!" She seized on that instantly. "But they would have studied me in some other way, would they not?"

"They would have asked you to share memories—"

"Memories for their storehouse. Now let us see . . ." Simsa dropped the rod across her knees and leaned back a little. "What can such memories consist of? My own of the Burrows would have no meaning for them. Thus they would have summoned that other and strengthened her, fed and nourished her, until she was and I was not. Is that not so?"

"What do you want?" he queried in turn. "Do you want to be of the Burrowers once again, to shut from you all the wonder and freedom and—"

"No!" Again she rolled her hand into a fist, thumped it painfully into the ground beside her knee. "But you—you cannot guess how it is—"

How was it, then? For a long moment she was caught up once again in that outflow-inflow of identity change which had been hers in the ruined temple. A warm richness spread through her. "Come . . ." It was a whisper. "Come—be—whole!"

So easy—a surrender that would be so easy. But beyond

that lay what? All the fears of the Burrows were cold in her, rising to blank out that gentle warmth. She would no longer be what she had always been, and even more then would she also be a prize to be fought over.

"Zasfern understands." Thom's voice reached her only dimly. "Talk with him, with any of his people. While you fight so, you are denying half the protection you say that you need. Was it you or the other who escaped the ship? No matter what you do now they will believe only in her existence, not in yours."

She knew that he spoke the truth. One of her enemies had been killed—but what was one among a number? She knew only Kuxortal, unless she unleashed the Elder One, or awoke her. But men were alike across the stars. They hungered and they knew greed on other worlds just as the lords of the upper city in Kuxortal maneuvered and fought openly and in secret for advantage over their fellows. She did not know whether the Elder One had powers enough to keep her freed from such demands and she wanted— To learn the height of power she would have to surrender herself, and to that she was not agreeing.

"So there will be other officers and other Greetas, and these among the Zacathans, too?"

"I think not. They are old, they live much longer than any other race or species we have found among the stars. To them knowledge is great, for they are the guardians of history, the stories of many empires which have carried conquest from world to world, of races who knew the stars before my own developed. Yet the Forerunners—of them they have only bits and pieces, mainly guesses. To Zasfern you would be a treasure to be guarded with his life—but only if you are willing."

"Think on this Zacathan lord of yours, picture him. . . ."

For the sake of knowing a little of the future she would dare so much. She saw Thom's eyes close, felt for herself the inward turn of thought. He was concentrating with the skill that made him what he was—one in search of the always new.

Between them was a stirring of the air, a stirring she could see more than she felt. At the center of that stir there was something materializing—Thom's thought? No, the power of the Elder One was at work again. Perhaps as much as Simsa that other was curious, was near desperate to discover who had inspired Thom and meant so much to this space rover that he risked death in service.

That fog-thing might well have been fed by the haze which was ever-present here, but it gathered substance enough for her to see.

Humanoid in that it had a manlike body, legs and arms clearly defined one from the other. But there were webs between the fingers, and on the scaly round head there was an upstanding crest of ribbed skin which wavered a little in the air as if it acted as antennae to reinforce sight or thought. The features were saurian in outline, with teeth surely meant to rend and tear flesh. There were no eyes in those dark pits—or else Thom's thought did not supply them.

Only for two breaths, no more, did she see that; then it was gone and Thom opened his eyes and let out a deep sigh of relief. There were beads of moisture on his face, shining on his ivory-colored skin as if he had been weeping.

"That was Zasfern."

How could he be so sure that she had seen anything? Apparently he believed she had.

"You have showed me his outer shell only." Simsa rose abruptly. "I must think." In spite of the eyes she was sure watched them from the underbrush, she strode away from the cave, along the roots of the cliff, battling one thought against another as she went.

There was a breeze moving under the trees, not to form any more specters out of Thom's past but to cool her body. Then Zass cried out from overhead and came to take position on her shoulder. Thom really believed in his mission and in this lizard-faced humanoid he served. Of that she had no doubts at all.

She crossed the empty ground at the cliff's foot to set her back against the bole of a tree and relax. But the thoughts that were crowding in upon her were like sharp-pointed thorns from some vine ringing her around. Surely her escape from the ship had been prudent? Who could be sure what outré weapon they might have used to cow her into obedience or drive all consciousness from her. Thom believed in his own truth—but that was not hers.

Simsa found herself listening, her head turned slightly to the north. The hum of a flitter! Thom was so sure they would come hunting him. But if they found nothing, or only indications that the other machine had sunk, would they then linger? And if they went from this world . . .

For the first time something other than the nameless and unsorted fears of the girl from the Burrows ebbed, and she was confronted with something else. Spend the rest of her life here in this valley? She stared about her, wondering. Never in her life before had she accepted imprisonment—she had been wary enough to escape it when she had run the Burrows ways. No matter how strong the door barrier of one of those underground dwellings had been, there had also existed bolt holes, the secrets of which were jealously guarded. It had been through one such that she and Thom had made their way to freedom on her last night in Kuxortal.

There could be bolt holes aplenty here, also. But what lay beyond? Only the seared, scored land which could support no life such as her own. That was so to the north and east—there remained south and west.

Intent on driving this new set of shadows back into oblivion, Simsa rose and began to walk, determined to make a complete circuit of the valley wall.

Once more she found the flight of steps down which they had come. She shrugged off any idea of another climb to the cliff top as yet. There would just be more rock, though twice that had been broken by crevices which might lead to caves such as they had left her to shelter in, or perhaps even to the mouths of passages—she marked each carefully in memory and continued.

When she reached a fringe of vegetation beyond which she could hear the play of water, she was sure that the fountain she had discovered on her first visit was there. Simsa then became fully aware that the cliff side here showed a number of indentations—shallow yet forming a pattern that ran horizontally and not vertically as if meant for a ladder out. These were so rounded of edge, so worn by time, that she could not be sure of any of them or their meaning. That they were not just intended to be decorative she was sure.

A little ahead the cliff burgeoned out in a wider curve, cutting into the valley itself. Here that pattern was not so faint, so worn. It consisted of a number of holes of equal proportion bored into the stone in clusters, but in few of those did the same number of holes appear, nor were they arranged in the same grouping.

Old Ferwar had been an avid collector of scraps of parchment, of any bits of stone bearing a strange design that could be writing. From her earliest essays into Burrow combing, Simsa had been alerted to find such, and many a sweet or copper piece had she earned from her old guardian when she'd brought one back.

There had been a number of scripts of different kinds on those fragments out of the past—wriggling lines running without a break across a crumpled bit of rotting parchment, or words set out in stone, often broken in the middle and the rest missing, in some tongue she was sure even Ferwar did not know. Now she was certain that what she saw was an inscription of such importance that it had been painfully and carefully drilled into the rock.

She rounded the outer bend of the invading rock point and once more faced the darkness of a break in the wall. The edges were uneven. It was apparent that the same hands that had carved a message into stone here had been busy again.

But at the midpoint of the stone arching above that entrance was something more than mere pitted stone. Nearly as badly worn by time as the rest, it hung there, blind-eyed and anonymous. It could be intended either as a warning or a welcome. The triangular head of one of the valley inhabitants was depicted, eyes not to be mistaken, many times life size, and with the effect of a never-sleeping sentinel.

With a hand gesture the girl suggested to Zass that she invade that dark space. But the zorsal refused with a whimpering cry. Nor did Simsa herself want to go ahead. A temple, a palace, a prison—it could be one or all three. It was not in the least like the residence of that moundlike erection at the valley's core.

She sniffed. Temples usually, to her Kuxortal-trained nostrils, burned some forms of scent. There was no sound of any movement, no sign of any path recently used here. For there was a clear drift of leaves, dull brownish through death, right across the entrance.

All peoples, Simsa had learned enough from traders to know, were jealous of the dwelling places of their gods or objects of power. For a stranger to enter such without the proper ceremonies was sometimes merely another and very unpleasant way of committing self-killing.

In spite of every suggestion her mind made, there was another part of Simsa that would not let her move on past this place without learning more about it. Step by cautious step she moved toward the entrance, and, as her feet crushing the dried leaves gave forth the smallest of crunches, she halted between each step to listen, turning her head from right to left.

Also she held the rod well up and gave full attention to the horns. There was no warning heat, no coming of the light. Judging by this, there was nothing of alien power housed inside.

Zass chittered in her ear and was ill at ease. Still Simsa could not break that compulsion which sent her on, over the threshold into the darker opening beyond.

As wide as the doorway was, it proved to be funnel-shaped, narrowing steadily on both sides so that to go forward she had to enter a passage that must have been designed to admit only a single one of the valley folk at a time. Being lesser than they in bulk, Simsa walked easily.

There were no breaks in the walls that closed about her—no doors into dark, secret ways, as there had been in that other chill passage she had entered. Here, sheltered somewhat from the weather, both walls were studded with pits or the holes that could be warnings, exhortations, even hymns to be sung—or thought—to some greater form of life.

The small amount of light that entered here from the valley was shortly gone. Simsa faced the dark with no light from her rod to supply her. Zass's whimpering cries grew stronger. Yet the girl received no clear warning from the zorsal, only that there was something here the creature did not like. Simsa paused, waited for a long moment, curiosity and prudence at war. Then she opened her mind in the way she had learned to do since the Elder One had come to her.

Thought quested ahead far faster than she could have run. And encountered—nothing. Or was there too *much* nothing? Simsa considered that thought silence carefully. She had discovered a mind shield on board the ship and at the port before they had lifted. Most of them the Elder One had contemptuously considered childish attempts and had let Simsa know that if she wished, they might be penetrated easily, not that the girl had cared to try them.

But this was, in its way, very different. As Simsa considered why she believed so, the Elder One stirred. It would seem that she also could be moved by curiosity. Because there was more than just that emotion moving her; On sudden impulse, Simsa stood aside—not waiting to be overtaken by that other—to afford the Elder One a free passage through the channels of her mind.

There were wesps of pictures, none of which she could seize upon long enough to clarify—buildings, places out-of-doors—temples, fanes, sanctuaries which the Elder One knew. Some with powers still there—others lost and forgotten, the powers dead with the people who had worshipped them.

Then came a delicate kind of prickling—yes, Simsa of the Burrows had been right. This was not one of those forsaken shrines—something waited ahead. Or did it slumber long past an awakening? The dark silence was far too deep.

She was not surprised when the moons glowed with their tip lights again. Zass was suddenly silent, enough so that her head brushed against the girl's cheek with every small snorting breath the zorsal drew. Once again, but for the first time since that hall when she had rushed into what she'd thought was completion, Simsa was with the Elder One, not pushed to one side, a spectator in her own body.

Those inscriptions on the walls were thick here, the lines of pits crowding in upon one again. Then they came out of that passage into a cavern or hall which was so large, so cloaked in darkness, that the rod's light was no more than a feeble candle end, showing no more than a few steps before her.

To venture out into the middle of that, away from the small sense of security that the wall itself gave, was hard. But Simsa had courage to match the Elder One's now. So they came to a large pit in which no fire burned, nothing stirred. Instead of light the depression was filled with fold upon fold of thick black, and when she lowered the rod and went down on one knee to see the better there was a heaving and a stirring of that dark as the sand had heaved and been troubled by what dwelt beneath.

"Sar Tanslit Grav!" The Elder One's words—or call—or greeting—echoed, with each echo growing the louder instead of diminishing, until Simsa wanted to cover her ears with her hands and could not.

"Sar!" As if that were a command which could not be disobeyed, the roiling of the dark grew. Faster spun the layers of it beneath.

Up from the heart of that troubled mass of nonlight came a long finger of the same thick blackness. And finger it was, as much as one upon her own hand, marked by the joints, a pointed nail on its tip—and yet that finger was near as tall as she.

It had risen straight upward and Simsa waited, shivering, for the hand to appear, but it remained a finger elongating itself as it rose. She caught another flashing picture from the Elder One of a finger that had once so risen from a grove of trees to beckon, and she shivered throughout her body, waiting for that to beckon her, knowing clearly in the same way that if it did so, she must follow.

It was beginning to incline in their direction.

Simsa flung back her head; in her upraised hand the rod twisted and turned. That reaching finger quivered—flashed out. Hallucination? But what had triggered it?

As she had done when the furred one began her spelling to bring down the flitter, so the girl began to hum, and that thrum was in some manner picked up by the rod and intensified. There was light now, fountaining forth from the rod itself, drawing a circle of radiance first around Simsa and then reaching out to encompass the pit. In its core there was the flood of black quiescence now—but only for a moment. As the hum grew louder and the light stronger, the pool of dark began to rise again within the stone cup that held it. There was a compulsion in that sound Simsa did understand. As if sound itself could accomplish that which she would believe only hands and body strength could bring about.

Once more the Elder One cried aloud through her lips:

"Sar—sar . . . Grav!"

Something broke the surface of the pool. It was not a giant fingertip reaching out to seize what it might crush upon the rock. No, that which was relinquished slowly, reluctantly, was a vast mass giving forth a stench that was not of any organic thing rotten, but rather like the smells Simsa remembered from the spaceport, from the ill-running machines that her own people—or the people of Kuxortal—did not know how to tend properly.

The bulk of it was nearly at the edge of the pit now, the blackness bearing it up. Then it washed forward so that Simsa had to leap back and away to escape the wave that brought it and then receded, leaving what it had so borne to drip ooze on the rock flooring. The Elder One moved her forward as a game piece again to stoop and touch the light of the rod to the black slime the thing was shedding.

There was a flash. Fire, which was like honest flames burning, ran outward from that touch, ate greedily at the ooze and drip until all she could see was a huge mass of burning stuff, from which she staggered back coughing as the reek of it bit into her lungs and brought tears from smarting eyes.

12

The fire ran fiercely, then smoldered into dark patches with dull crimson gaps where the flames still ate as they died. This was no machine such as she had seen in company with the off-worlders, nor did it have anything of Kuxortal in it. It was a mixture of solid plates and branching ribs—a carcass and yet not one of any once living creature.

Made by the hands of others, not born by the way of nature. Simsa was ready to swear to that. What it might be she could not have said. There was a rain of sooty bits flying from the structure as if it shook itself to get rid of the last fragments of that covering.

"Yathafer . . ." It was not Simsa of the Burrows who had breathed that name, though her lips had shaped it. Just like all her touches with the Elder One, this was only part of a mystery. Looking upon that blackened thing, she saw it not, but rather a glider, soaring great wings against the sky, a sky

177

that was not curtained in the haze that covered all here, a sky clear and faintly golden. And he who so winged about, using the upper drafts of air to raise and ride, he was—

The faintest of memories struggled in her. No, it was not *his* name she had spoken a moment earlier. It was that of what he did—wind riding, freeing himself from the clutches of earth to soar and swoop and be borne by the breeze's will. He was—

"Shreedan . . ." Yes! That was the name, but where was that flyer? And how on this world of bare rock and traveling sand had Yathafer wings come to be hidden?

That congealed darkness which filled the basin had drained away. She looked into a black hole where nothing moved. Yet before her was that which was of her people. Why had it arisen to her now? Or was this merely another manifestation of the rod she carried—that it could in truth control all of the foretime?

Tarnished metal showed as the black ashes fell away. She saw the body swing and it was intact, as were the wings which had been closed, one overlapping the other, following custom when the Yath men stored their craft.

Deliberately Simsa edged by that craft to point the rod straight down into the basin from which the thing had so emerged. There was no trickery or hallucination leading her to see what was not. She had already reached forth a hand and flicked more ash from the wing edge, felt the solid metal. So—what else might lie hidden below? Simsa was certain that the rider of the Yathafer could not lie here. Or, if he did, his life had long since fled. But she wanted to make sure—she had to! The excitement was like a lash laid about her shoulders, driving her along to more discoveries.

Fixing her mind firmly on the problem, the girl summoned whatever else might lie before that was or had been made by hands. There was no roiling of the dark in answer, even though the light of the rod grew stronger as she poured into it all the energy she could summon, reaching a peak of power that she had held only during the ceremony with the valley seeress when they had summoned the whirlwind.

She saw the sides of the bore, and then there was utter dark which swallowed up her light. Either this was strong enough to hold any other prey, once it had been alerted, or else there was nothing left.

At length Simsa realized that she was expending power for nothing, and she loosed control and concentration, turning instead to the machine so oddly revealed to her. Slipping her rod into the girdle about her waist, she caught with both hands at the edge of the folded wings and gave a slight pull. There was no resistance; rather, the wing moved easily. Nor did it fall apart as she half expected it might. So she was able to push it before her, shedding more of the ash all the time, heading for the entrance.

Her people— Simsa of the Burrows stirred. No, the people of the Elder One—they must have been here, too, in the forgotten past to leave this artifact of their own design. But why had they come? She was sure that this was not the world that had first shaped them—what might the Great Memory be able to tell her concerning that past?

She had to learn so much. From the star rovers of this day she had plucked some things, but always warily, afraid ever to reveal herself entirely. On Kuxortal she had been an exile; was here another exile of her race awaiting discovery? Know— she must know!

As the girl drew the long-hidden flyer into the open, she found herself no longer alone. Here squatted the strangely banded one who had been—who was—the Great Memory, renewed within the egg, ready once again to serve her people. On either side of her, two of the larger valley females reared high, their upper limbs free and claws clicking softly.

Behind them was another party. Thom, on his feet, his arms stretched wide apart, each of his wrists in the claw hold of a valley guard, stood there. Though human or near human eyes could read no expression on those large-eyed faces, still Simsa was sure that peril was with him. Yet she did not pause—or that one within her would not let her, as she came fully into the open, pulling the machine behind her. The light caught painting on the upper of the folded wings—a spiral of blue flecked with glistening stars which did not appear to need direct sun rays to give forth diamond splendor in flashing points.

"What—drew—you—from Pool of Forgetting—" The mind search of the Great Memory quavered in the girl's head.

"That which was of my own people," Simsa replied. "How came it here?" Even as she asked that, her mind was busy trying to storm a door stubbornly shut against her. Blue—and diamond-bright sparks—those had a meaning— what—how—who?

The Great Memory, still on all fours, advanced a single step. Her head turned up at an acute angle so she could center the gaze of her eyes on Simsa, hold the girl so. Simsa was aware of a steady and ever-strengthening thrust against her, as if the Great Memory would encompass her about and squeeze from her what the alien wanted most to know.

"You have troubled the Place of Forgetting." That was a forceful accusation. "Why?"

"Why do you seek to renew memories yourself, egg born?" countered the girl. "I was led here—" How true that might be she did not really want to know, but she suspected much. "To learn what pertains to me and mine. Now I lay upon you, Great Memory, by your own rules, tell me of this thing—or who flew it, and where, and when—and why."

There was a long moment of silence. Then:

"Since the pool has given it back to you, your power is attuned to it. Back—back too far, egg sister, rides *that* memory. Perhaps there was another like you who came hither in an earlier day—perhaps once this whole world was like the valley until death struck and struck."

Simsa stiffened. A cold wind might have blown out of the cavern behind, lapped her around.

"What death?" she asked, and feared the answer. Had those who had nurtured her fought these? If so, how could there be any link between them except one of enmity?

"Out of the winds it came, and it shut away the eye of day. It slew all which lived upon the earth, save here where there were the ancient guards and they held, but it was many times the toll of egg years. Marsu was Great Memory and lived out ten egg turns thereafter, for there were none born after the death of the Eye and its closing for long and long who tested for memory. After her there was Kubat, but the memory was less and, it was only because Marsu could not take the egg again that Kubat, the most promising, went to the first transferral—five egg times was *she* Great Memory. After her there were many, many." Tshalft clicked one set of foreclaws as she counted out those names that perhaps even memory could not string like beads in a line forever.

"And there was never any end to the curse of those from the sky—only here. Thus it was."

"Those from the sky . . ." Simsa pushed herself to ask the question. "They were kin to me?"

"Not so." She was so ready to hear otherwise that the girl gave a small gasp of relief. "For there were those like unto you who strove to aid when the Death came. And death claimed them, also. One alone won to this place of strength and hiding, and in the fullness of time he fell into the great sleep, nor could he tell us how to rebuild his egg so he could come forth again. Then we took that"—she indicated the flyer with a claw—"to the Pool of Forgetting, which holds all that is not to be brought to memory again. It was a thing we had not learned to use and memories without use had best be forgotten."

"And from where did he come, this one who could fly, and the others with him?"

The answer she expected came clearly:

"From the sky also. But they wrought not in death. They treasured life whether it be in their form or another's, which was not true of those who brought the death. Long ago that was, a very small memory, and one which fades even when the egg renews."

"Of what manner of form were they—these dealers in death?"

The Great Memory swung a little about, her claw stabbing the air in the direction of Thom, where he stood prisoner.

"I have searched the Great Memory and the lesser, the

newer and the elder. And this one bears the look of those who brought the Death.''

"He may look like those," Simsa countered, "but they vanished with all their kind over the years. This one comes from a new people, a people which are as nestlings late out of the sack. He is not your enemy.''

"There is a memory like unto him," the other repeated stubbornly. Her thought sending was gathering strength, and, with it, Simsa could sense an impeccable will which carried memories through years of hibernation and rebirth in the service of the rest.

"Memory is of two parts," returned the girl slowly. "There is that which shows itself a picture, there is another of the inner part no one can see—save through experience. He may wear the guise of that ancient enemy—but he is not kin, nor blood, nor bone of theirs.''

It was difficult to judge what impression she was making when she could not read any facial expression. Now she added what she hoped would be further proof of Thom's innocence.

"This one found me egg-bound, as I might be said to be, on another world and helped to loose me. Would he have done so had he been as those who strove to destroy your world?''

There came no answer from the Great Memory for a long time, too long. As when they had stood in the valley before, she and that one who had controlled strange forces, there came the sound of a flitter faint in beat but not to be mistaken—seeking—from the northeast.

Thom might have heard it first. His head was up so his eyes could search the haze.

"Again they come in search." It was one of the guards who broke mind silence first. She pointed with her mandible-set lower face toward the cliff. "He calls and they come!"

"You set up a direction call?" For the first time Simsa spoke directly to Thom. "One to lead them here?"

He shook his head. "There is one such on the flitter. It was triggered when we crashed. That will be their direction."

She raised her hand and Zass, who had floated out of the haze to take position on her shoulder, now stepped onto her wrist. Simsa looked deeply into those feral eyes. "Watch— watch—unseen—" she beamed an order.

The zorsal flapped wings and cried out hoarsely, then sprang into the air, soaring deep into the protective curtain of the mist, beyond the power of Simsa's eyes to follow her. Now the girl looked to the Great Memory.

"If it is the flitter which they seek, perhaps they will find it—but the rocks hold no track prints to bring them here."

"They will not come." There was something very final about the Great Memory's reply. "If they seek, they may find." She turned her head but a fraction, but Simsa knew as well as if it had been shouted aloud that these would make use of Thom as a final answer to any such search—that a safely dead body could not betray them.

She moved swiftly, pushing past the Great Memory. The rod's tip flicked from one to the other of those claws that held Thom's wrists and the creatures dropped their holds, their limbs falling as if stricken powerless against their furred bodies.

She need give him no orders. He was already alerted, leaping from between his late captors to Simsa's side, his hands instinctively on his weapon.

"No!" she uttered aloud with force. "These have good reason to fear your kind. Prove yourself peaceful and you have a chance with them."

Then her mind spoke to the Great Memory as one to bargain.

"I, too, have a quarrel with those you hear. But this one is not of their kind—"

"He came with them!" was the instant interruption.

"Yes, but in his way he is also subject to them. Now he is free of them, he wants no more of their company." She was improvising. She turned her head a fraction to speak directly to Thom.

"They will destroy those whom they believe seek them out here. In the past some humanoid race blasted their world into what you have seen. My people, they tell me, who were here for another purpose, were also brought down. You must be dead—if you want to live." She smiled grimly.

He rubbed one wrist with the fingers of his other hand.

"If they do not find me . . ." he began slowly in trade-lingo, and then continued, "Yes, it might be so. If they locate the flyer and I am not in it, they can believe that I was—" His mouth moved in a twist of disgust and she knew what he thought—of the tentacle-things that had taken so eagerly what fortune had brought them. That they were killers and doubtless carnivorous she had no doubt.

"But . . ." He stared at her very directly. "If they believe me dead as Greeta, they will lift ship and—"

"You shall remain." Simsa beat him to that protest. "How soon will they lift ship?"

He shrugged. "There will be nothing to make them linger

here. They will believe you dead, also—once they have seen what preys out of that sand trap.''

She looked about her, needing no thought contact with any of the valley dwellers to realize that these would do nothing, except perhaps, in a grudging way, provide some shelter. To spend a lifetime on this scraped rock world which had a single cup in which life could continue . . . Her own desires protested that. How much harder must it be for this space rover trapped now with her, whose whole life had been given to the stars?

"Perhaps . . ." She was forced into this. It was her fault that he was here and she no longer believed that he had any desire to wish her ill. "Perhaps you might be found—"

"Dead!" That word snapped into her mind and she knew that the Great Memory at least could dip into her thoughts and see what lay behind any speech her lips shaped.

"Not so!"

There were small sparks dancing at the tips of the rod horns. Fight—no. She had no wish, no will to blast any from her path except those mindless things that swelled and crawled from out the sand. The valley inhabitants had every right on their side.

"Not so," she repeated firmly. "Cannot memory be altered, or is this not the skill of yours, Great One?"

There was a moment in which she could read startlement and near repugnance. To alter memory for this one would be breaking belief in all she had been taught to hold the most sacred.

"You do this?" There was vast distaste in the question she threw at Simsa.

"I can make one see what is not. . . ." She held the rod

between overlapping hands. "Look you!" she commanded, pointing to a rock, a battered crown showing between two tall growths. The girl concentrated, narrowing both vision and thought to a single thing. On the rock there sprawled one of the yellow horrors from the sand holes.

With a loud mewling sound one of the guards launched herself at the apparition just as Simsa broke the picture. Claws scraped bare rock. There was nothing left of that obscene intruder.

"It is forbidden to play so," the Great Memory flung at her.

"I do not play—I merely showed what can be. If people can be so deceived as to sight, they can also be deceived as to what they *have* seen."

"Forbidden!"

"To you, not to me," Simsa responded. "Let me take this spaceman to a place near his people. Then I shall set in his mind a crooked memory, and this I can do."

"But you shall have still the real memory, and what if that is read?"

The Elder One drew up Simsa's body proudly. "These are but children when it comes to forces of the mind—and memory—Great One. Do you believe that such as they stand any chance of winning of any thought I am not ready to supply fully?"

"And what do we know of you?" The Great Memory was far from being convinced.

"That I have helped. Ask your singer of storms what I did with her. Those who so labor cannot close evil thoughts and show only the good. So do I swear upon this—" She held the rod higher. Now from the tips of the horns there shot larger sparks of blue light which flew as might some insects into the air about them. "I swear that I mean you and your people all that is well—I swear that *my* memory shall be locked while I am with this one from the skies—and that when he is set among his people once again he shall forget all except what I shall allow him to recall. And—"

Once more the sound of flitter, this time nearer, beating steadily, not circling as the first one had done. Zass came out of the haze and sought a landing place on Simsa's shoulder.

"Flying thing—bad sand—goes—" She lifted the words from the zorsal's mind.

"They are centering in upon the place where the other flitter crashed," she told the Great Memory. "We may have but little time. Shall I do this thing or will you tie here one so different that he will leave an ill memory behind him—of death when it should have been life?"

The Great Memory hunched herself together and the claws on her forelimbs clicked. She had closed the passage of communication between them and Simsa stood ready with the rod. That she must defend Thom now was a duty she wished had not been laid upon her. Though she did believe that he had not been party to the exploitation that the others of his kind had wished for her.

"Your flitter," she told him, "is centering in on where the other was sand-trapped. I trust that they are armed—"

"Yes. What are you going to do?"

"Return you to them," she said promptly.

"And you?"

"That choice remains mine. I have not found such a

welcome among your kind that I care to repeat a trip with them.''

"But you cannot stay here!'' He looked around him. "There may not be another chance for you to go off planet.''

She glanced at the winged machine which had come to her call. There had been no escape for the one who had once used that to soar above the barren rocks of this trap. Yes, it was a trap, but it was a trap she could master after a fashion. The trap that was offered by his kind she doubly feared.

"You know nothing of this world,'' she evaded him. "What have you seen of it? A small portion only.'' She held the rod between them; those awakened tips sent their spill of sparks in his direction, forming a wheel about his head, spinning faster and faster until they made a ring of fire. She felt his instant response of fear, of danger signaling his body into action. But he only had time to jerk his head a little.

Then he stood statue still and Simsa began her task. There was again the flitter sliding into the morass of the bubbling sand. This time no compulsion of hers brought him out of the wrecked ship; rather, it was his own effort that led him to leap to the ground from that unsteady and perilous perch.

He wandered, he fought the blobs, but Simsa was not a part of the action which was all his. He had that implanted with a skill that haste did not destroy. He did not come into the valley—he had seen nothing of those who dwelt there. Instead he had sheltered on that rock perch reaching out from the ramparts of the cliffs and there he had been successful in fighting off two attacks of the sand creatures.

Skillfully the Elder One wrought and Simsa herself knew a chill of fear at that skillful weaving. She was sure that this was not the first time the other in her body had worked such a transformation of what had been into what she wanted it to be. Would she someday turn on Simsa and blot out all memory of the Burrows—of the real girl she had been? That was what she had feared from the first, after her exultation at finding the Elder One. She might resemble that other to the last fine silver hair springing from her black scalp, but she was not the Elder One—not yet.

Thom stood quietly, staring straight before him. What he was seeing, she knew, was not the valley but that plateau of rock, and he would keep that in mind only until they were back at that point.

"You have changed his memory." The Great Memory drew farther away from her.

"I have saved his life," the girl answered. "But there is one thing more."

She brought to mind another vivid picture—across the barren rock just below the height on which he perched was a broken body, and though he tried fiercely to reach it, to beat off the two creatures who dragged it away under the sand, it was gone, all that black skin and silver hair swallowed up forever. To satisfy the valley dwellers, to end any more questing, Simsa gave him her death.

13
•••••••••••••••
•••••••••••••••

While Thom was still bemusedly reliving the false memory, Simsa and two of the guards took him back up the valley stairs, sent him down cliff and across the rude dam of the fallen rocks by the uniting of their will. Simsa watched him stagger up and out upon the tongue of rock. Between him and her now there swirled a thickening tongue of the haze. Those who found him would not seek farther, not after he had told his story. He was only a darker shadow in the haze this far away and yet she stood watching him.

By the beliefs of the valley folk she had done wrong. She refused to let herself think ahead to what the future might hold for her, another exile on the seared world as had been the one who had soared and flown in earlier, brighter days. Could those wings still bear one aloft—and, if they could, would she attempt such a flight once the skies were free of the flitter whose beat overhead sounded louder and louder?

Zass descended to settle on the girl's shoulder, but she did not need any message from the zorsal to realize that off-world aid was at hand for Thom.

The mist distorted but it could not entirely hide the figure of the man on that rocky rise beyond the cliffs. Out of the haze a flitter settled in a straight line from the sky. There was another aboard who swiftly lifted the overhead cabin cover and leapt from the machine to front the waiting spaceman. They were too far away for voices to carry, to know what Thom reported. Would her conditioning hold the false memory? Simsa's body was tense as she waited, half expecting them to turn in her direction. But they did not. A moment or two later, Thom, the pilot's hand on his arm to guide him, returned to the flitter. With a rumble it rose from the rock.

As it was swallowed up by the haze, still Simsa waited, listening, telling herself that what she had done was the best for all concerned. Whether she had lost the favor of the valley ones or not did not matter. They had shown no desire yet to exile her from their refuge, and thus she still had access to life-sustaining supplies.

She stroked Zass, taking comfort in the rubbing of the soft antennae-crowned head against her cheek. In so much she had this one to cling to. And—for a moment she hesitated, wondering if such a thing could be so, could she also by will alter her own memories—wipe from the past all that would make her restless and discontented with this cup in which she might well spend the rest of her life?

There was something within her—and it was not the Elder One—that suggested she had chosen wrongly, that her place was out there, no matter how suspicious she was of the motives of Thom's people, seeking new things ever. The

Elder One? No, she could not now contact that one. Her fear of being bound in this prison was that of the real Simsa—and to it she could not yield.

Once more in the valley she sought out that cave in which Thom had been sheltered for a space. She curled on the mat bed place where he had rested, willing sleep. It came. The last thing of which she was truly aware was the nestling of Zass beside her, the small warm body against her own breast and the low, contented crooning of the zorsal lulling. . . .

She must have dreamed, but none of that dream aroused her into the wakefulness. Her arms were about Zass so tightly that the zorsal protested and nipped at her hand. There was the dampness of sweat along her body and she was breathing in short gasps as if she had been running for her life before a hunt of vastly superior power.

Her mouth was parched—she might have been shouting for help for hours. Help against whom, and why? Simsa did not believe that the valley dwellers had sent such a thing upon her. No, it was the old, old law which Ferwar had so often quoted to a heedless girl child. Use any power for the bemusement or ill of another and it recoils upon the sender a hundredfold. Only she had not meddled to Thom's hurt, but for his own safety!

She licked dry lips. Outside the narrow niche of cave the haze was that of day. Here it was easy to lose all sense of time with no real night or sunlight to measure it for one. She might have slept for hours; the painful stiffness that hit her as she tried to move suggested that indeed a lengthy time had passed.

Zass was gone, doubtless to hunt. She herself was well aware of a hunger pang like a knife thrust through her

middle. Crawling out of her rough shelter, she rose to look about.

A short distance away, purple globes hung from the boughs of a tree scarcely more than her own height. She headed toward that, uncaring at the moment whether the fruit would be safe eating for an off-world digestion or not. It was full ripe, giving forth a good smell as she twisted a globe from the branch and mouthed it.

Sweet, but with an undertaste of tartness, its juice trickled down her dry throat. Nor did she hesitate or wait after the first mouthful to test safety. Having eaten a half dozen of the fruit, she sought the water basin.

There were three of the valley dwellers there, drawing water into jars. At her coming they each glanced once at her and then pointedly away, making it very plain that they intended no contact. Simsa waited until they were gone and then fell on her knees to draw her sticky hands back and forth in the water before drinking. Once more that liquid invigorated her.

When she had done she started in the direction of the structure that was the heart of the valley. Twice more she met the furred ones along the paths, both times having to take a hurried step out of the way when it became apparent they had no intention of giving any room to her. It was as if she had really become one of those illusions she had spun in the ship's cabin to deceive those who would spy upon her.

So plain was this nonrecognition that Simsa found herself rubbing her left hand along her body in reassurance that she was indeed there and that this was not a very realistic dream. She never remembered eating or drinking in a dream before— but that was no promise that one did not indulge in such satisfactions for an ailing body. Perhaps, as Thom, she was

afevered and walked only in spirit. No, such a thought was
foolishness—she was alive and awake. But that she was so
overlooked meant trouble—trouble that could only come from
what she had done to Thom.

Memory meant much to those of the valley—so much that
it would seem they bred or carefully trained their holders of
recall. To force wrong memories on someone who could not
withstand her power to do so . . . yes, to them that might be
worse than the outright slaying of the prisoner. Yet she had
done just that as much for them as for him. Surely they did
not want to have descend upon them those such as the officer
and Greeta, greedy to learn the secrets of others. Now after
Thom's false report the ship would take off, and there would
be no future exploration—they were safe.

"Not so!"

Simsa wheeled to face a wall of the thorn-bearing bush that
walled the pathways before she realized that the words had
not come to her ears but into her mind. And the thought,
from the force and vigor, that was the Great Memory, or else
she who had raised the whirlwind with the Elder One's help.

Simsa hunted the first opening in the thorn bush and
pushed through it into another of the clearings. No water
basin here, no glittering shards of broken egg—only four of
the people. There sat the Great Memory, the claws on her
forelimbs turned into fists to better support her more upright
stance, and beside her the priestess or chieftainess who had
summoned the whirlwind. It was she who made an abrupt
gesture with her right claw which brought Simsa to sit cross-
legged facing them all.

"They are gone—back to their ship—back to the sky
which gave them forth," the younger leader thought with

vigor. "Yet you remain and, from the memory of the one you favored, you took much. Why is this so?"

"That he and those with him would do as you have said—leave this world and seek no more. He now believes me dead."

"As you showed to him—" the Great Memory came in. "Why?"

"Have I not said—some of those are my enemies." Simsa was puzzled at that question. "Believing me dead, they seek no more, leave your world. Is this not what you have wanted, Great Memory?"

Leaning her weight heavily on her left arm and fist, the older one uncurled her claws and, on a patch of hardened clay before her, drew with claw tip a series of what looked like a mixture of coils, one slipping into another. Between these she then inserted deep holes, boring claw tip well into the ground. When she had done, she looked to Simsa almost triumphantly, the girl thought, if such faces could reveal any clear expression.

All four of them were still, waiting. Undoubtedly she was expected now to answer and she did not even know the question. Was that muddle of lines and pits on the ground a message? If so, she had no chance of reading it and there was no value in suggesting that she did.

She pointed with the tip of her rod to the lines. "I do not know the meaning," she thought slowly and, she hoped, with emphasis enough so that they would believe her.

But even as she tried such communication the rod shifted in her hands, turning, with forces she could not fight, to interact with a portion of the pattern. And there uncoiled in her head—

"Hav bu, san gorl—" The words were not only fiery pictures in her mind, she was speaking them aloud. The Elder One knew. This *was* a challenge, a contest of wits and of memories, something that had happened long and long ago and had never been forgotten. The rod trembled in a game of sorts, one in which the stakes were very high—even life or death. And it was a game that was not native here to this forgotten valley. Who had he been—what had he been—that lost, air-soaring one who had sheltered here until his years ran out?

She had a flash of picture, of ebony skin and a mane of silver hair, of brilliant jewels aflash as bodies crowded about two who sat and played for stakes that would condemn one, exalt the other. This was deadly contest and she came to it with a riven mind.

Again she was not one but two. One of those twins was impotent, a prisoner who could only watch a game not of chance but skill. There had been the flyer and another— another whose face she could not see clearly, blurred as if the years between them had worn it away, even as wind wears away in time the hardest of stone. Yes, the player and the flyer—it was his fears and longings that she touched upon for a moment of keen despair.

Exile. That was the price for the loser. And what the gain? Change—a change he could not allow. This was all a whirl of shadows Simsa could not pin down to understand. Mind power against mind power, desperation against rising triumph. Even as Thom had been molded and sent forth to play *her* game, so was this one being mastered to act for another. Knowledge was power—and power was the ultimate goal for any living creature.

Wrong! Deadly wrong, something struggled within the prisoner Simsa. She had known the power of the half-barbaric nobles of Kuxortal and had taken her chances with it. There had been the infinitely greater power of the spacepeople, and here—here of the valley dwellers, the power she had dared to draw to her to turn Thom's life from one path to another. Power—always power! Within Simsa a bitter struggle began, a lost one, for the Elder One was clearly awake and lying in wait. *Her* game had been successfully played out. She was not going to withdraw now.

There was a tearing within the girl, a supreme effort which the watching Simsa thought she could never have made. But she was no longer the one who triumphed, but rather the winged one. And the fire that filled her was the flame of his despair and need. Only a glimpse of that ancient battle was she allowed, and then—

Darkness—though she knew that she did not sleep or wander in any land of illusion. There was a spark of light. She somehow felt the pain of that which held her stretched upon rock, bruising her body. There was the ship—not the one that she had voyaged upon and fled from. The faint outlines she could see rising from that core of light were different. A ship lost in time—an ascension from this world even as Thom and those who had rescued him would go—if they had not already gone. She was left alone as it climbed skyward, then she was alone again. What had she won? Doom for herself and perhaps no victory for those for whom she had fought her battle. She willed the dark to close utterly, that she might know that all changes were past, that she must live and die as that sky rider had chosen.

She must have passed out of the far time into the now in

sleep. For when she again battled with the dark, it was to awaken in that same shallow cave where Thom had sheltered. For a long moment she did not move but lay there staring up at the ragged rock about her, wondering at what she had seen and its meaning. Time, she had all the time in the world now to think about what she had done, perhaps not once but twice, as the wheel of the great years made its slow turning. Had she indeed savored the last confrontation of the flyer and one of his people? One who successfully built false memories could never again trust his or her own.

She pulled herself up to look over that valley of life in the midst of so much desolation. Simsa had always prided herself on her self-sufficiency, that after she had been able to walk, talk, and feed herself, she had progressed steadily toward full independence. Yes, she had shared with Ferwar, but somehow the old woman's attitude toward her had been one of very casual interest after she had dinned, beaten, bullied the fiercely independent girl child into abiding by the only rules that meant safety on Kuxortal. Simsa had come these last dozen years or so to think of herself as one free, in no way forced to another's ways.

Certainly she was now freer yet, for there was not one left on this unnamed world who could lay any task upon her. The valley people were apart—she could expect nothing from them, save perhaps food, water, and this rock over her head. She had the zorsal, but, as long-lived as Zass might be, she would not spend too many more weary years here.

Nor—Simsa sat the straighter and her mouth became a determined line—nor need she stay here, either, to dry away into nothingness because she was forced idle. What had she seen of this world after all? The fissured plain in which the sand rivers flowed and this valley! But that was not a world, only a very small part of it! There was nothing to prevent her going forth again, with supplies she could cull here, to advance her wanderings. What had brought that first ship, the one of the flyer, to this world? The impression lingered strongly with her, *not* at any nudging of the Elder One, that there had been a reason—no casual or unplanned voyage as her own coming had been. There was no suggestion either that that exile had fled and been followed as she had been. Therefore, let her see what had drawn those others, even though time might have nearly erased all signs or traces!

The need for action had always been a part of Simsa of the Burrows. Perhaps it had also tinted the musing of the Elder One, for the girl was aware now of a flow of strength, as if that other part of her agreed, was impatiently pushing her toward faring forth.

It was dawn. Her "sleep" must have lasted hours. And she felt the refreshment of her body. Simsa swung out of the cave, went down to the fringe of the green stuff.

How many memories did she ride now? She tried to control the shaking of her hands. How was it she knew that if she broke from the parent branch two of those paddle shaped leaves and pressed their edges closely together, she could fashion a bag, one strong enough to carry water? Her hands were already busy at the task, and cautiously she sought the Elder One. There was a blotting out there, so— *No,* she had had a hard enough time as two people. She would not welcome a third—the hovering identity of the flyer—too!

Yet when she was fully equipped with two water bags filled and sealed and fruit she had examined critically that it be not too ripe, she felt free enough. East lay the river of sand, the plain over which she had come. Nowhere in that journeying had she seen more than dead rock and a blasted world. Not east, then—west? And that direction also had the advantage of being away from the landing place of the Life Boat and presumably where Thom's ship had also set down.

She whistled as she headed toward that stairway up the cliff. Zass came winging, circling about Simsa's head, complaining with a hoarse croaking at what lay in her mind. Yet the zorsal made no move to remain behind but went with the girl as she climbed steadily to the top of the cliff wall again. That flyer, he had not even had such as Zass to bear him company—she was not as bereft as he. Now she set him firmly out of her mind as she tramped along the lip of the cliffs working her way to the opposite side of the valley.

The haze was always thicker in the morning, and as she looked down into the cut before leaving she could hardly see the highest crowns of the trees. They had their own protection from discovery. When she tried to stare ahead, she could see only a little. But it was enough to locate where a fall of rock gave her a place over which to scramble down.

That river of sand flowed here, too, but in the place below the land slip it was narrow. Rocks tumbled to leave only a space over which she dared to leap. When she crossed, she stood staring keenly about her. To find such an aid to return to the valley was almost as though her mind had moved the cliffs to achieve it. But she must be aware of the ease which the haze might spin her around into losing it. She reached among the debris of the slide that had fallen on the other side of the stream and picked out any pebbles she could find that held a glint of pure yellow. Several such had been fractured in the crush of the fall and gave off bright sparkles from their scraped surfaces. These she chose first.

Setting, as she hoped, straight out from the valley toward the unknown west, Simsa left a train of such pebbles, one dropped every twenty strides. The haze was thinning and seeming to rise into the usual ceiling across the plains, so she could see and easily avoid any of those threatening fissures. Though the air was warm and the rock actually hot under her feet, there was still no sign of the haze thinning enough to let in the sunlight.

Zass now and then raised in flight which carried her out of sight into the dimness before she returned again, to settle with complaining grunts on Simsa's already talon-scratched shoulder. There was no way of marking any hour, just as there appeared to be no end to the monotony of the other plain. She had chanced upon no more rivers of sand, and even the fissures were smaller and farther apart.

A seam of reddish yellow drew her to one side. Simsa hoped she had chanced upon a vein of more of the colored pebbles she could use for markers, as her supply fast diminished. But as she came closer she saw that it was not a mineral that had raised that streak of color but seemingly a plant—the stems thrusting upward from rosettes formed by flat leaves against the stone, some tipped with bright red blossoms. At least she thought they might be termed that, though they were not open, but rather appeared as tightly rolled cylinders.

There was not only plant life but insects which hovered over those blossoms, unrolling tongues almost as long as the rest of their small bodies to thrust those deep into the flowers. Zass croaked with interest and then appeared to decide that the feeders were too small game for her to exert herself to catch.

More and more patches of the vegetation spread in streaks along the rocks, and those were rising in a ridge—a slow upward slant which did not require too much exertion to follow. The insects whirled away on almost invisibly thin wings and then resettled as she passed. Now there was a second type of growth, this anchored on the level surfaces of the stones over which she climbed. Like the things that lived in the sand streams, this was deadly to the smaller life-forms, for it threw out long limbs patterned with thorns. Simsa strove to avoid their seeking claws. Not all travelers were so lucky. Simsa caught sight of a white blob on the ground. One of her jumps to avoid a thorned lash rocked the blob and sent it spinning over so she could see the eye holes of a skull, though she had found no other land animal hereabouts. These remains of a victim made her look more carefully for any trace of such life.

At one or two places the moving tentacles of the plants raised such a barrier that Simsa leaped the obstructions, fearing to feel the rake of entrapping thorns on foot or ankle as she crossed there. The larger they were the more she could foresee trouble if she kept on a direct course. Then both plants ceased growth abruptly as a last jump landed her on an expanse of what appeared to be ebony-hued glass, so that she slipped in spite of desperate efforts to keep to her feet, sprawling forward, luckily out of reach of those flailing vegetable arms.

Zass had leaped to wing and now screamed with rage at what she considered hard usage, drawing Simsa's attention aloft. She sat very stiff, her eyes trying to take it all in, even as she had studied the ruins of faraway Kuxortal.

No vegetation masked this place, but there had been far worse things that had happened to what had manifestly been a building or collection of such which in size far rivaled Kuxortal itself. These buildings had—melted!

Before her, walls were half-buried in a hardened ooze of their own substance. Simsa could see that beyond the pools of glasslike puddles were other walls rising three, four, and even more stories high the farther her eyes peered through the haze.

Nor had those higher and less damaged walls been fashioned of stone. Even in the hiding of the haze they gave forth a metallic sheen, bearing no resemblance to the rocks on which they stood.

Unlike the mound buildings in the valley, these had openings at ground level where they were not entirely melted into formlessness, and they were closer to those she had always known. A palace, a fortification, a city so built that only narrow paths, rather than broad roads, linked or divided? She did not know what she had chanced upon or—

Within her was such a strong surge of memory that the Elder One won control before she was prepared for any battle.

"Yi—Yi Hal . . ." The strange words she uttered echoed from one building to the next, carrying on hollowly from where she faced the wreckage, deeper and deeper into the mass before her, until she almost thought she was being answered by something hidden in the haze.

"Yyyyiii—Hhhalll . . ."

But in truth all she heard was Zass's scream as the zorsal planed down to sit on the nearest mound of circled rock.

Pushing against the cry of recognition came another memory. Not—not home—never Yi Hal again. Only this which looked enough like it to deceive at first glance.

Simsa clasped the rod of power closer to her so that the points of the twin moons pricked her flesh. Never again Yi Hal! Simsa of the Burrows had no site that had ever been truly a safe and happy refuge from the world—but now she wept the Elder One's tears as memories lived, flickered, died, and she sat alone in the ruin of what was not Yi Hal.

14

●●●●●●●●●●●●●●●●
●●●●●●●●●●●●●●●●

That abiding trait which all her life had drawn Simsa into adventures, and had at last landed her on the present glassy puddle, stirred. She was curious. This was a dead place and still it drew her. Back on Kuxortal she had grubbed for those finds out of the past that had been hidden in the walls, the roofs, the footpaths of the Burrows. This was like the Burrows, a dead place—waiting— To offer the intruder what? She rubbed the grief tears away from her cheeks with one hand. What did she know of that past? she asked herself fiercely. Nothing! Let the Elder One mourn if she would— Simsa was more intent upon what lay before her.

She crawled on her hands and knees across the puddle of glass until she could lay hands on stone. The footing was slick and she had no mind to fall.

Thrusting the rod into her belt, Simsa worked her way along the walls, part of whose substance had bubbled down into such a trap. There was the opening of a dark doorway, and, calling on all her boldness, Simsa pulled herself within. Whatever, whoever, had built this massive pile had been not much taller than she. Half-consciously she had been watching for some carving, some runic inscription or sign. The dead city she and Thom had found on Kuxortal had had such. And there were those ancient eroded markings on the cave wherein she had ventured in the valley. But here were only walls, and a kind of grimness which began to dampen her eagerness.

The room within was as bare of wall as was the outer husk. Yet the surface was so smooth to the touch that she could believe that if the melting blast had not licked within, there would have been a metallic surface that resembled the rock without. Dull gray, then—

Simsa went into a half crouch, her rod jerked forth and up in threat or warning. That shadow before her aped her own stance. A long moment of tense apprehension passed before the girl realized that what she did see was her own reflection as hazy of outline as if a tendril of the mist outside had been drawn with her.

She walked forward, ashamed at her reaction to such a thing. Putting out her hand, she touched the surface of a mirror far more accurate in reflection, as she slid her palm along against that other hand raised to meet it, than the polished metal discs so used on her own world.

She studied the figure she faced. Her hair floated free—a ragged mass of fringed stuff about her head and shoulders. Her black body faded from sight in the dim light of this place. All she could see clearly was that hair, her jeweled kilt, the rod in her hand. Her other palm against the surface slipped slowly to the right, then met nothing. A moment later she discovered that the mirror was not part of the wall, but rather screened another door behind. The purpose of its setting puzzled her. Could it be that those who had once lived here announced their presence as visitors by such reflections cast on the mirrors?

She slipped behind that barrier to go on. Oddly enough, though she could not distinguish any source for it—there was light of a sort, enough to show here the blank walls of a passage. Zass croaked and gibbered impatiently from her shoulder perch. Her neck at full length, her antennae weaving back and forth, the zorsal projected a feeling of excitement, as if they were approaching another grove of trees from which she could take her fill of prey. It might be that in this dark gloom Zass remembered the warehouses on Kuxortal where her kind kept under firm control the destroying vermin that scuttled among the bales.

Of course—the wuuls—the rod swung in Simsa's hand before she began to marvel at that snatch of other memory. Something that was gray white and crept upon its belly, though its weak-looking legs could ensnare and hold with the force of a trap—the wuuls that feasted on both the dead and the living.

"Wuul?" She questioned aloud that picture which had snapped into her mind.

She answered herself with an exclamation that was both fear and irritation mingled. Wuuls came from no place or time, she, the real Simsa, knew. Yet the thought of them was so real she found herself straining to hear, slowing her own pace to watch and listen—for what? Something that must have lived elsewhere and long since become dust. This was a memory of the Elder One or that other which intruded now and then—the flyer.

If traveling through this place was going to release such scraps of alien memory, it would be better now to retrace her steps and leave the ancient pile to its death sleep.

Only when she had decided that this was the choice to be made, she discovered that she had no means of carrying it out. Simsa was not aware of the Elder One in control, of the haunting of that other exile. To all tests she was in command—of her thought, perhaps, but not her body. That carried her on into this ruin which was fast becoming a maze.

The corridor she followed split and split again. Never did she hesitate at such a branching. As if someone far stronger than she held her by the shoulders, she was turned briskly right or left to march on.

There were openings along the sides which might indicate rooms, even as in the underground ways the valley dwellers had traveled. But none of those did this pressure allow her to explore.

Twice she was out-of-doors for the space of a stride or two, always sent ahead into another door across that narrow way, until she began to believe that this compulsion was carrying her directly into the center of the city, fort, palace, or whatever this pile had once been.

There were no relics of its earlier inhabitants—just the smooth corridors down which she was marched, some straight, a few curved. Then the way began to slope upward, not by means of any stair, but rather at a gentle incline, until, at last, Simsa emerged into one large room without a ceiling. There was no sign of metal above—perhaps this had always lain open to the haze of the sky.

In the center was a pool, an oval with a raised rim about it. And even though there was no sun to bring out their glitter to the fullest, Simsa could see that it was encrusted with a pattern of brilliant stones, gems to which she could not give names.

Making a half circle about the rim of the pool were seven chairs—or thrones, for they possessed such adornment of jewels as to be the seats for great nobles. And inlaid on the back of each was a symbol.

Simsa's rod swung up, the horns of the moons pointing.

"Rhotgard." She signed to the first in line. Then—

"Mazil, Gurret, Desak, Xytl, Tammyt, and Ummano—"

She threw herself down on the pavement before those thrones, the rod falling with a clatter across the stone, as she folded her arms over her breasts and weaved back and forth in the age-old way of one who mourns. Within her, fear swelled to panic—to such terror as left her weak.

She could not control that which was in her. Never again would she be what she was. These others—the Elder One, that other faint shadow who had done the naming of names— they were taking her over, tearing at the small part of her that had kept an imperiled freedom. Once she had welcomed knowledge, now she would flee it—rip the encroaching others from her own flesh if she could.

Instead, that which used her to ride into life was making her crawl in her debasement, reach out hands to the water of the pool—for there was water there, though dark and turgid so that one could not see what lay below it. This liquid which lay in that place—her skin was roughed by the breath of her terror—still she could not draw back.

Her fingers forced themselves into a cup, swooped to

break the quiet surface of the pool. Somehow she had expected the water to be night black as it lingered in the hollow of her palm. But it was green like that of the valley, cool but not cold.

Her mouth opened against her will as her hand rose to her lips and she drank. That liquid which seemed so cool in her hand—as she sucked it up from her palm it was bitter, warm. She might have been lapping from some muddy-bottomed footprint left on a trail or from one of the ill-smelling, stagnant seepages in the Burrows. Still she swallowed, unable to reject what she mouthed, not only that but two palmfuls more.

Bitter and hot in her mouth, growing hotter in her throat, pain spreading into her middle, until she bent over, both hands pressed to the place between her breasts where that pain seemed to eat the worst—dully at first and then with quick thrusts. Poison! A safeguard that had been placed here and to which her own disturbed inner struggle had treacherously guided her. She would die. She fought to raise a hand, ran her finger into her mouth, her throat, that her own muscles could eject this torment. But her hands were no longer hers—they betrayed her, too, though they continued to nurse her middle.

The *High Cup*! Memory warred with memory. It was as if her own trick with Thom had certainly been forced back against her again. Of old this was—not to show pain, to sit unbowed, serene as the poisonous fire ate, until her own talent—power—could render it harmless.

She uncoiled from her huddle of anguish on the floor. Even what was left of Simsa of the Burrows understood this. She had been struck, perhaps past any defense, but the girl who had made her way through all of Kuxortal's fetid trails unmarked, cunningly, able to face down any opponent—save Ferwar—that girl came out of hiding to give her the pride to stand straight and tall fronting the chairs of the missing. She seized upon another trail of memory. An initiation of sorts, though the reason for such had long ago disappeared and what she had to offer might be worthless now. If she had been tricked and trapped . . . well, she would play it through!

Fight what gnawed within her, not by the rubbing of hands, the voicing of any pain cries—fight with the mind! Just as she had wrought with Thom, overlaying true with what was false, so must she work here. There was pain, but it was fading. By concentration she forced her trembling hands away from her body and held them before her as they shook, and the fingers writhed with the torment. No—that was growing less. Think it off! Instead of the poisonous draft she had swallowed, she forced into her mind the memory of the drink from the pool in the valley, sweet, cool, refreshing. That was what she had drunk.

Hands, be still—fingers, together, no more trembling, no clawing at the air. Coolness within her. Sweat gathered on her forehead, dripped down like the first of a spring rain from her chin and cheeks to her breasts and shoulders. The effort wrenched at her almost as much as the pain had done. And, behind it all, those two others waiting—the Elder One, the flyer, waiting for her failure.

Which would *not* come!

Do not think pain—think something else. What was the greatest thing that had ever happened to her, which made all the rest of her life small and mean and of no account? That moment when she had stood before the statue that might have been her own likeness, when she had first known the Elder One and—welcomed her! When she had first believed that she could rise to greater heights, before the seed of doubt had been planted, before she had known what she might represent to others.

That was the hour, the endless moment in which she had been really whole, when she had been born anew into a different world. Here was a place that was also one of birth—

The thrones were empty. They had long been so. There were none in this hall to judge her endurance, her talent, only herself. Simsa held her body tensely erect as the gnawing within her twisted and tore afresh. Do not think of what might have been, what once had been. Think of now and the next moment and the next. Pit all her strength against the pain and that which was meant to finish her if she did not fight it.

Her hands—they no longer trembled. She willed them to spread fingers, contract them again. Her arms next—the scarlet thread of torment which ran like the blood in her veins. That was *not* greater than she could bear. This she had done before and came out the victor.

She? The other she. Who was she now—the thief from the Burrows or that much greater one? Both—they must be fitted together or she was left with death. No! Keep her mind free from such a thought. This was the place of trial. She did not shrink from what it would bring her.

Arms—the hot pain was less, surely it was less. Feet—the heat within them that seemed to char its way outward . . . There was no heat! She would walk where she willed and there was none who could say her nay! Not now, not ever!

The twisting pain within her, coil upon cramping coil . . .

She stood, she breathed, lived, and she would continue so. Simsa drew upon that pain, surveyed it as she would a new road opening before her. Simsa! Not the Elder One, not the thin shadow of the flyer—no, she herself. She was one!

"One—one—against you!" She shouted aloud her defiance to the empty thrones, to the shadows who had once been seated there. "I am Simsa!"

Even as she turned all the power she possessed to hold on that thought, using it as both shield and sword, the dark roared in upon her. Nor was she aware anymore of her body which held the pain, of anything save that she was Simsa and so she would be, unto death itself.

There was no pool, the thrones were gone, she moved through a place of drifting shadows. They might have been those cast by others like herself, wanderers in a place that was meant for searching—and which she must best not by aimless hunting but by finding!

Some were like trails of silver smoke with no hint of form about them. Others were faceless men and women floating. The shadows of shadows that clothed them were strange and varied from one drifter to the next. Twice she was sure that she had sighted figures in spacer clothes, a woman in a robe of the desert people, and others—so many others. But she refused to be a shadow, refused even to look down along her own form to see whether she matched these lost and wandering ones.

Rather she put purpose to her own drifting, forged ahead as if to some goal. She had come here to hunt. Therefore, to be about that task as speedily as possible was what she must do.

Beyond the shadow people, arose—and then became tenuous wraiths of their own—buildings, tall towers, squat blocks, things of vivid beauty, darker structures which in their way threatened . . . The people, the kingdoms, the worlds—

Her hands moved and still she would not watch them, only fasten her mind on what they did. For in the air of this place of shadows her fingers moved with a purpose. On the air itself she sketched it—the rod with the sun, the horned moons in protection on either side.

That was no shadow; rather, it was light, dazzling light that did not hang there. It was moving, her guide through this place to whatever lay beyond. Perhaps this was the world of the dead. She had heard many beliefs and fragments of beliefs in the past. There were temples aplenty in Kuxortal, and Simsa had shunned them all in her time—finding in none of them any stronger will than her own.

What lord ruled here—or what lady? She need not ask. The answer was ready in her thoughts: Soahanna.

Again at the thinking of that name the orb before her sped the faster and she urged that which was left of her to course behind it. It appeared now that the dark in which all those mist figures moved was thicker, was attempting to slow her, hold her back.

All her will concentrated on the one thing, that there was a power, a will, a force here which she must front and upon that fronting meant all that would save her from becoming one with the other drifters.

The dark thickened. The other shadows were very few now and only the thinnest trails of mist were visible. Yet the orb pointed her on. And she would go—the stubborn will that had been born in her from the beginning held her to that.

The last of the searching shadows was gone, dark pressed

tight on her in another form of pain. But that dark could not hide the orbed light nor stay in its forward flight. Perhaps that symbol in some manner cleared the way also for her. She continued to concentrate upon it fiercely.

There was no more dark. Here was the arid, scraped plain, the river of sand, the fissures that hid death. She was back; yet there was a kind of lifelessness—if rock and sand ever held life—and the orb swept ahead.

Was she going back? That fleeting thought nipped at her concentration. She expelled it firmly.

No more rocks and whirled sand—this was the ship cabin in which she had known, being spied upon, that she must take charge of her own life again. Only a flash of that—

The spaceport at Kuxortal where the whole of her story had started, where she had seen Thom and marked him down as the perfect customer for her bits and pieces dug out of the past.

That, too, was gone in a rippling as if it had all been painted upon some curtain which was now yielding to a rising wind. Here was that other city, ancient beyond the counting of Kuxortal, the city in which she and Thom had found the smugglers, and that field of spaceships which would never lift again—the city in which she would discover, on her own, the Elder One.

The hall now, the very place where she had made that discovery. Only she did not see it as one who entered but rather from the dais as one who had waited and waited for years out of time's flow. She was the Elder One!

And again there was a shadow—one who came even as Simsa of the Burrows came to wonder and to break time's lock. The globe swooped toward that shadow. It disappeared and she was again able to move. But she knew her first meeting had been the right one. When she doubted then, she had unconsciously attempted to rend something that had been meant to be sealed. Yes, she was Simsa, but—

By the light of the orb she could see the two hands that reached forth. She seized upon the rod and brought it to her. This was what she had sought—this was the binding beyond any cutting of bonds.

Dark again, but now no whirling trails of mist people. Simsa opened her eyes. She lay on her side, her knee nudging the rim of the poison pool. Pain . . . she waited for the pain to begin again. Then she realized she had learned, she had gone beyond. The very ancient final test for travelers had been given her, and she was the victor.

Yet when she tried to pull herself up she was very tired, as worn as if she had hiked for days or labored past her bounds of energy.

She heard the scream of Zass and the zorsal spiraled from the sky haze overhead, to claw a hold on the back of the middle throne. Suddenly, in a rising tide of laughter, Simsa felt within her relief from all that had happened since she had found this chamber.

"Ha, Rhotgard, wherever you may be—see what wisdom has now come to seat itself in your place." She moved too fast and grimaced as limbs that had been cramped protested. Making a wry face in the direction of the pool of initiation, she pulled forward her own leaf bag and took a swallow of the water she had brought with her.

The pool was no longer calm, glasslike as a mirror, nor was it aripple. Still, through its depth so that she caught glimpses now and then, she saw movement, the movement of those shadow people who lived (if they lived) now apart.

Her fruit was overripe and smelled as though it were close to rotting. But she conscientiously ate it, and, with the water, it was summoning back her strength. Zass walked the length of the throne seat and came so to peer into the pool herself.

She flung up her head so that her antennae tossed like plumes and spat—the ultimate in her gestures of disdain.

"Be not so bold," Simsa warned her. "It is a test, but it might be more for an impudent zorsal." She scrambled awkwardly to her feet and then began stretching and bending each limb, turning her body this way and that. How long had the shadowland kept her? She could not tell—time itself was forgotten here. But the pain that had racked her was gone and what she felt now was only the complaint of cramped muscles.

She stooped at last and picked up the rod. Perhaps it had not shared her venture, but its essence had brought her through. It would be long, she thought, before she would learn *all* it was capable of in her hands, even though the Elder One was no longer pushed aside but shared the high seat within her.

With half recognition the girl looked around. She might never have trod the rock of this world before, but this chamber was familiar to her, a place that was to be found in every sector center where the Kalassa went. Kalassa—she had a name and with it a flood of memories which she banished for the moment. Time enough to pull upon those when she had not her own work to undo. That which she had wrought in fear must be broken. Such fears were like the drifting shadows, things now without any real substance at all.

From this world there was speeding a ship, and on board it

one with whose memories she had meddled. As the valley dwellers, she realized fully now what her fear had led her to do. She had made of him also two people, and who better than she could understand what that would mean to any living creature? He would dream and awake with bits of dream so real that it would shake him, his belief in himself. He would walk down some street on another world and see an object that would bring a flash of recognition; he would be talking to friends and suddenly wonder why he had used words . . . He would—

No!

If she had learned anything in this time of trial, it was that none should be two. Perhaps the memory self she had set on Thom would not be as known to him, as much of a burden as the one she had borne, but he was to be freed from even the shadow of a shadow.

She put aside her bags and set her improvised pack to one side. With the rod firmly in her right hand, she approached the throne nearest to her.

"By thy leave, sisterling." She had not said that aloud, but she was certain that it reached whatever shadow had once had form and had sat there judging. Seating herself forward on the throne, she passed the rod with a wide swing of her arm across the end of the pool nearest to her.

For the first time the surface of the water was broken by a troubling which sent wavelets skidding outward from an upsurge in its center. That troubling of the water brought with it a puff of odor—not as foul as one would believe could rise from a poisoned pool, rather one that made her think of a field on Kuxortal where she had once lain down under the sun of spring and spent a quiet hour such as those of the Burrows seldom knew.

Staring down into the troubled pool, she began tentatively, with some fear, which she quickly choked off lest it weaken her, to search. What she had done tied them. The Elder One knew and feared such ties. For if ill came of it, both the captured and the captor suffered. So it was with a sense of duty as strong as any order laid upon her that Simsa began her search.

First she visualized her Life Boat, how she had left it among an upturn of rocks that had the appearance of a forest of stone trees stripped of all save their broken boles. He had been there—it was what had sent him questing out across the rock plain. So—

"Thom?" No call echoed aloud, but such a seeking as this world, this galaxy, had not known for a thousand years' planet time—or more. "Thom?"

In the pool she used the troubled waters to build his reflection. So lay his dark hair—so were set the planes of his face, his slanting eyes—so had he looked with that intent study when they had sought the answer to the death that had lain in the ruined city for countless years, with the threat of returning to trouble life-forces again. There were his shoulders, wide under the tight-clinging fabric of his spacer's uniform, his narrow waist so supple when he moved— Bit by bit, calling her own memories of him to the fore, she built his likeness upon the water.

Now—she edged forward a fraction on the throne—*now* she must see him as he went from her the last time, wide-eyed but sightless for a time, his wound dressed with the rags of her blanket, his head still up as if he, too, heard the hum of the flitter come to take him back.

He was a man, no illusion that she might have constructed to save herself for a space. And because he was a man she owed him—Simsa fingered the rod, drew fiercely upon that other memory—a debt to be paid and only she to pay it.

Yet his shadow grew no clearer as she strove to break through the wall she had so harshly and strongly built to control his future. He was like those spacemen clad in armor whom they had fought together on Kuxortal, impervious to the very will that had sent him forth.

Thom! she demanded again.

He was gone!

The strength she had put into his summoning swung back upon her like a blow, until she felt as if the last thread of breath was almost driven from her lungs. She dropped the rod and caught with both hands at the arms of the throne chair lest she be thrown into the fury of the pool before her, whose contents seethed as if all the fires in the world were bringing them to a boil.

Simsa swayed again, braced herself. She had so strongly believed that what one had wrought might be also dismissed upon willing. But Thom—she could not even hold any longer to him at all! Hers the deed, and one she would have to live with.

That backlash of the power she had used was exhausting itself. She felt sick and giddy as she huddled in her seat, watching the whirling of the waters.

"Elder One." She did not cry aloud, but the petition of that name echoed through her spare, taut body. "Elder One?"

Wildly she threw open her mind, summoned—what, she did not know. Somewhere there was an answer. She had been so confident that she could break the bonds laid upon Thom. The valley people had been right in their judgment of her act. She had called forces she could not even put name to and now she would dare to try again—if she could—for her

will was a limp thing, drained of all energy, a feeble tool she could not depend upon.

The tumult in the pool was subsiding, and the haze overhead was thickening for night. Still Simsa crouched within the curve of the throne and Zass, perched on the taller back of the one in the middle, let out a small cry—a querulous one demanding attention.

At last Simsa gathered up the rod that lay at her feet, stumbled down and away from her perch. She caught one foot against her pack and would have fallen, looking at it dully. Then she gathered up her water bags, and what else she had carried, turned her back upon the pool and the thrones, and wavered toward the entrance that had brought her hither. Zass cried out again and flew a circle over the girl's head as Simsa took hesitant step by hesitant step, unaware of the tears wetting her thin cheeks.

She had been so very sure that she had at last come into her real heritage, that there would no longer be a cleavage within her. But when she had tried to project as she was sure that the Elder One had been able to do— Perhaps she had bested the Elder One in spite of herself. Sometimes that which one wanted the most slipped through one's fingers. And she had been for all this time trying to push away from her that oneness which she had first delighted in.

As she went Simsa made no choice of passage to follow. The long dimly lit hallways fed into one another, and she was so weary. Yet she could not rest here in the place of her great failure. Let her win out of this shrine of the dead, be again under the open haze of nighttime. That she wanted more than anything, now, with a dumb, inner aching. Twice the zorsal returned to ride for a short time on her shoulder as she

stumbled along. But whenever Simsa stood for a moment or two, supporting herself with one hand against the wall, Zass uttered chirruping cries in her very ear as if she would spur the girl on to greater efforts, as though she knew ahead lay something better than the gloom of these stark corridors.

At last a final door stood open and there was more light before her. She wavered out into the open, the stark-walled buildings behind her.

Here was a platform overhanging a dip in the contour of the land which descended in a series of wide ledges or steps into such a tangle of vegetation as she had seen in the valley. The buildings or building lay entirely behind her and she was free of its hold on her. Simsa crossed the first of those ledges and, on the second, as far from the door through which she came as she could go, she dropped to the stone, the zorsal taking off into the mists of the night with a cry that sounded like a shrilling of triumph.

There was food and water. Most of the fruit was too bruised and spoiled to eat, and she hurled it from her into the growth beneath. She allowed herself only a few sips of the water, not knowing when she would find another spring, and curled up; the weakness and fatigue she had carried as a burden since she came from the initiation chamber finally crushed her. Though there was only the hard stone to lie upon, Simsa drowsed.

An aching loneliness closed in, flooding her mind as the fatigue tore upon her body. Was this how the flyer had felt when the past was cut from his life and he had been left here alone? She herself had cut off her past deliberately, and now— Was it worth what she had done? That was her last thought before sleep, deep and dreamless, closed upon her.

15

Farther—out and out—she had tied a bond between them, surely she could ride that road to find him. The rod blazed high in her hands and the water in the pool now churned from side to side. Still, below its surface she could see an outline of a shadow—a ship—the ship that should have borne him away. But that was still standing on its fins, pointing skyward. Not off world yet?

Simsa pinned that shadow with part of her will, held it steady, as within it she sought that which she must find. There were living things encased, yes. She brushed past minds, impatient to discover what she sought. None of them— then where—

Thom! Of his name she made a cord of concentration, of demanding.

Thom! At last she touched! As Zass might use her claws to capture prey, so did Simsa fasten on that other one. Thom!

Did she dream? If she did, there was no memory upon awakening. It was Zass's shrilling cry that pulled her out of that depth. The zorsal walked up and down the ledge within an arm's length, her antennae weaving furiously. Plainly, she was disturbed or highly excited. It was midday by the look of the haze overhead.

For the second time Simsa had awakened so cramped and sore of body that it was a minor agony to move. Before prudence ruled again, she had taken up the leaf carrier that held water within—the other being already flattened and dry—and drank deeply to clear her throat of the dust of this place which still choked her.

Zass's talons clicked against the rock of the wide step as she came to squat before the girl, looking up into her face with an interest that demanded attention.

"Others—"

"Others?" queried Simsa. What others could there be, unless that wide stretch of vegetation to which the steps led was another inhabited valley. She tried to pick up from the in-and-out emissions of the zorsal's mind some hint.

But while she looked to Zass for aid there came another sound out of the haze overhead, one that made her drag herself up, striving to find the last rags of energy to carry her. Where? Back into the place of the long dead—or forward down the stairs into that green-gold covering? A flitter! She could not mistake that!

But Thom—surely he had been firmly under the altered memories when he had left her. When? Days earlier? In this haze it was easy to lose all track of time. What else would he do but quietly and obediently return to the outer world, wait for his people? There had been no break in the shell she had

built about him—that she could swear to. Or dared she swear
to anything? Hallucinations might have betrayed her instead
of him. Still, she was not ready to confront any off-worlder.

Simsa pushed a heavy lock of hair out of her eyes. She
made her decision quickly as the sound of the flitter grew
stronger. There was an odd glow on the haze some distance
to the north—as if the machine itself was emitting light in
order to break up the haze. Or perhaps these off-worlders
with all their bits of knowledge regained from the shattered
past could use some mechanical means to so penetrate that
curtain which cocooned this part of the planet.

At any rate, these tall bushes and trees ahead promised
better hiding. Were those aloft in the flitter to sight the
buildings, she was certain they would land, perhaps upon the
very ledge above her, for exploration. Her cramped body
protesting every movement, she started running for the end of
the second ledge where she had slept, then across the next
one. Three such she descended without seeing more of the
off-world machine than that spot in the haze, but the sound of
the engine was steady—a heavy beat—and it was moving at a
pace no faster than a walking one. They were spying below—
they had to be.

She had seen on screens within the spaceship pictures
taken from at least six different worlds. They had tried to
interest her so, she had thought, that she would not be aware
of their intentions concerning herself.

Her foot came down on a rotted fruit, perhaps one of those
she had flung to the winds earlier, and she skidded, flailing
arms to try and retain her balance. Her efforts brought her to
the right-hand side of that wide flight of stairs so that when
she fell it was not on the worked stone but on the earth

beyond. She had only a second to ball herself as well as she could. Then she struck with a jolt that drove the air out of her lungs and rolled on down until she hit against the thick stem of a plant that was tree tall and tossed its leafed head from the shaking she gave it.

For a moment she could only lie there. Somewhere Zass was airborne and calling to her. But she believed that the zorsal was wary enough to keep away from the flitter still, by the sound, cruising overhead. As soon as she got her breath back fully, paying no attention to bleeding scratches or abrasions, she crept on her hands and knees farther on until she was sure that she was under cover. Then she rolled over on her back and stared up at the leafed branches overhead trying to think, to subdue her rush of panic.

Why had she believed that the ceremony of the forgotten people had made her invincible? That independence which had been hers from birth had made her believe that she was a worker of wonders—

All right, let her now work one of those wonders on this hovering sky spy. Dared she try to reach any aboard that flyer with a talent that she admitted now she was untrained to use? Had it been her seeking for Thom at the hall of thrones that had brought the space rovers out again to hunt? Her foolishness was enough to shame her many times over. To attack an enemy when you did not know the range of any weapon that might be brought against you—to overestimate your own . . . Yes, she was a fool and they could be only playing with her in order to cow her into their hands to do their will with even less freedom than a zorsal on a flying leash.

Thorns tore at her shoulders. A vine, locked about her

throat, brought her close enough to the choking point to make her fight vigorously. But all this was under the reaching roof of the trees, and perhaps she passed unseen. Or did they have such spy weapons as could pierce through that leafy covering, center on any life-form that moved below? Simsa all her life had heard so many tales of the invincible machines and installations of the spacemen that she could believe anything might be true.

There were no paths here, or at least she had not chanced on one.

One path—just one path— She had no idea why that meant so much to her, unless it promised speed. What did she flee? Some reaching bolt of energy from that flyer overhead? The sound of its engine deepened, almost like the roar of a canzar from her home world.

Then there was wafted through the moist air that hung under the larger trees such a putrid stench that the odor alone halted her mad flight. She eased back on her heels and sent a short mind call for Zass.

Deep within her mind something stirred. This was no longer the Elder One awakening—she *was* the Elder One— but that fragment of other memory was not hers by right. She gained a fleeting mind picture of what? Not a reptile, for it had no marked head, only a round pulpiness of wriggling grayish body. Then it raised one end of that body and she saw an opening, a dark red maw surrounded by two circles of crushing teeth.

"Wuul!" Not her own memory—that other's wuul! She snatched at what that other knew concerning the loathsome crawler.

Killer—with no mind to be touched, to command, although those who had built the ruins behind were long gone, this creature of their own world was free and coursed the mangled planet left to it.

Panting, Simsa set her back to the nearest of the tree-sized plants, readied the rod. The smell was choking in its nauseating heaviness. She retched in spite of her fight for control.

"Wuul!" Frantically she tried to gain more from those two who had accompanied her to this outpost—the Elder One, that far-faded remnant of the exiled flyer. All she received in return was the wariness of one, the stubborn desire to fight of the other.

She purposely tried to put the hum of the flitter out of her hearing and settle upon the here and now. The bushes were rent as a tree fell to her right. Small things skittered and ran blindly, most of them making for other trees. There was a sullen crunching as the tree that had been downed thrashed from side to side. Its root end was being furiously and thoroughly shaken.

Simsa slipped back, putting the bole of the growth under which she sheltered between her and the thing. Then she turned and ran back the way she had come, branches lashing at her, blood welling from cuts across her arms and legs. There came the crash of another tree just as she reached the end of the vegetation that lapped about the bottom ledge. She threw herself out and forward on the stone and scrambled somehow onto the next higher.

That blot in the haze hung just about her now, pulsating. Another tree went down—she gasped and made it up a third ledge. Of Zass there was no sign and she hoped that the zorsal would have intelligence enough to keep off from both the flyer and her own position.

Once before she had seen Zass and her two sons fight and kill a monstrous thing out of the wilderness. But that was on another planet and the thing was not a wuul. The stench of the creature preceded it as another tree, this time on the very edge of the opening where lay the bottom ledge, crashed.

Wuuls could eat anything, even rock that bore such lichens as she had seen before the other entrance to the ruins. But all would infinitely prefer meat—and she was meat!

She thought of the ruins, of that maze of hallways. No, to be trapped in there by a wrong turn or choice—that she dared not chance. Not in haste now, but as one making a last stand against impossible odds, Simsa stood ready. She held the rod tightly—it was her last hope. Yet both the Elder One who had carried this and the lost flyer feared the wuul.

Into the open pushed a mass of gray, unwholesome flesh, heaving as the jaws ground along the tree it had brought down. It had no eyes—

No, meat it hunted by heat, the other part of her memory supplied. There was no way she could shut off that kind of body radiation which was drawing the thing. She was a large section of meat raising in it a stronger call. The pulp of vegetation leaking down it, the thing raised the blind end that faced her. The roll of the jaws never stopped, though now they spat forth green sludge which had filled its mouth, preparing for the far more attractive prey ahead.

As it reared part of its forelength from the ground, the end weaving back and forth, Simsa could guess that it was near the length of four or five of her own kind, monstrous as the things that bedded in the sand river.

The things that bedded in the sand river?

No! Hadn't her building of hallucinations failed drastically once with Thom even after she had given her full stretch to their weaving? This thing had no eyes. It sensed by other means, although it seemed now to be in no hurry, as if it savored her disgust and strictly controlled fear as another part of the feast.

The things that bedded in the river—

Simsa ran a tongue across the dryness of her lips. That would not leave her mind! She could not be sure whether it was the last stupid thought of the Simsa who had been—or a part of the new Simsa who was.

The things that bedded in the river! But she must withdraw, put aside thought and fear of the wuul, if she would try this. And that might condemn her from the start.

Nevertheless—the people of the Elder One, her people if she believed that she was of a freak birth that brought into being one of the true Forerunners. If all Thom had said was the truth—if that were so—and if she had passed the initiation by the pool, then—

Simsa deliberately closed her eyes to the weaving forepart of the wuul, to build in her mind the largest, the most active of those things that had threatened her from the fissures of the rocky plain or had crawled from the river. Its leprous yellow hide, so swollen of belly until it seemed all stomach and guts with only a vestige beyond, save for those suckerpocked arms—many of them—reaching out.

"Come," she demanded, putting into the order all the strength she could summon. If the fissure thing was as well protected as Thom—if she failed—

Something stirred. She touched and clung with her thought, prodded and pricked. It was not too far away! Perhaps there were fissures here as well as on the plain, having each their inhabitants.

"Come!" This time she reinforced her mental order with a shouted word.

Along the side of the slope, away from the ledges, there was a crumbling of earth. Lumps fell outward, there was a trickle of running sand which edged out and down.

Why did the wuul hold off its attack? She wondered for an instant or two, then realized that she must concentrate instead on that which she called.

More and more of the earth was slipping downward. Then, as if an inner dam had given way, a whole cascade of the running sand washed aside two lumps of earth near as large as her own body. From that hole which had hidden there waved the end of a tentacle.

Shock struck Simsa. Somehow she had not believed entirely, she had expected failure in one small part of her. Now her will soared like the battle cry of fresh troops sent in to make or mar the victory.

"Come!"

She waved the rod in a wide gesture as if she would clear the way for the creature. The bubbling, flowing sand was now a torrent. Tumbling rather than swimming in it came that which she had called. Big—the biggest she had seen.

It passed the ledge on which she stood, reached, with the flowing of sand, the small level space between the last step and the beginning of the vegetation. And either through some motion of its own or because it had been carried by the sand and strove now to fight its way loose, it crawled forth on the ground, hunching its fat bag of a body together, sending forth reaching arms.

The wuul moved at last, a slow, relentless descent of its head, the mouth extending open to the farthest extent, ready to engulf the sand-thing. Tentacles tossed, slapped across and around the pulpy gray body.

There was no sound aloud, but the wuul projected a fury, a pain.

The wuul was gone!

On the flattened vegetation the sand creature sprawled. Simsa could also sense its vast surprise and rage. There were the trees downed by its opponent. On the air still lingered the reek of the wuul—only it was gone as one might snuff out the flame of a lamp!

Then she knew!

Trick—someone in that hovering flyer had worked this trick, one as intricate in its way as the false memory she had so carefully built for Thom. Something (she still believed in the expertise of these makers of machines) had been in her head!

Simsa snarled as might any cornered animal. In *her* head! Someone had learned the first fear of the Forerunners and had turned that thread of memory against her—to hunt her into the open where she would be easy prey. They must have tested her in turn—for the wuul had waited, they had waited to see what she could command against their threat. And easily had she supplied them with that answer. She should have been aware that she was being fought with weapons close to her own, laughed at their wuul and kept in hiding.

A tentacle caught the edge below her. She doubted if she could send back this threat of her own, for it was real and its hunger was not a set part of any trap. As the wuul had seemed to do, it must have sensed or smelled her, for it was showing a surprising burst of speed, using its tentacles to draw itself up toward her, having reversed or perhaps never started the charge toward the wuul.

Raising the rod, Simsa felt more sure of herself. At least she had met this terror before and won past it. But as she strove to empower the rod she realized that once again there was an end to the force she could summon to activate it. Her course of action since she had entered the ruins might have made the past clearer, but it also showed that the Forerunners—the Elder Ones—had not been invincible.

First, with all the force she could bring to bear, and then with mounting fear, the girl tried to confront the sand creature. There was no crackling lash of fire from the twin crescents—only a small glow. When she attempted to use her will, the thing seemed impervious to any mental contact. Although it had come to her call, it was too alien or perhaps even too far down in the scale of fire—or on another wave of contact—for her to reach it.

The puzzle of that she had no time to solve. She retreated to another ledge up as the thing drew itself along the rock surfaces below. Then, bursting into her mind like a thrust of spacer energy, came her name!

That sudden hailing unnerved her for an instant, almost too long, for a tentacle aimed to the farthest extent the creature could reach scraped just before her toes, and she scrambled back.

"Simsa—up—quick—"

Thom? No, that had not been the spaceman. There was no clear picture in her mind, and still the communication was sharper, stronger than the young off-worlder had ever used.

This was someone who trained in the same methods she had so painfully learned from the Elder One at the beginning.

So forceful was that order that she turned and took the last two of the ledge steps, returning to the forefront of the ruins, at the swiftest pace she could muster. As she wheeled, for she had no intention of being driven back into the maze of the ruin's corridors with a sand dweller at her heels, there struck straight down from that reddish spot in the sky, which marked the flitter, a spear of light such as she had seen enough of in the spacers' records to recognize. It was a weapon much like her rod, yet not powered by will and concentration of personal energy but by units of captive force upon which the people of the star fleets depend.

It struck full upon the sand-thing, which writhed as smoke, black and evil-smelling, rose from it. The thing lost its hold on the ledge to which it had just pulled and fell back, its tentacles waving vainly, striving to bring its fall to an end. It crashed at last into the sand flow which had formed a shallow pool, puddling just at the foot of the ledges. There it lay, still heaving a little, only half within the flood.

Now! Simsa had no desire to stay for Thom or this other and more forceful personage to land, if landing was what they intended. The ruins offered her a way out. The wuul—

She stopped within the overhang of the doorway. That brain—that stranger—had driven her, as a man drives fleexe does out of the pasture, out of the trees. What was to prevent him or her from driving again? Wuul in the open was one thing, but wuul underground—or in narrow hallways—hallucinatory or not, was something she could not bring herself to face.

16

Simsa placed her back against the stone wall of a square-cut pillar that sided the entrance to the ruins. She forced her breathing to slow, brought under uneasy control fear and anger. There had been too much heaped upon her. The experience in the initiation hall, her flight from the flitter overhead, and the supreme effort she had made to produce the sand dweller had weakened her. She need only look at the barely lit points of her moon rod to tell her how little she had in her to withstand whatever was coming.

Not Thom—that last message had never come from the off-worlder. Then who? Certainly not that officer who had seen in her talents—or supposed talents—a chance to renew his fortunes. And Greeta was dead. Who?

Not to know the enemy was one of the worst things she faced. For if one knew, at least there was time for some preparation. She had none except her own stubborn wariness and realization that she must not yield to any off-worlder.

The flitter was going to land. That blot in the haze resolved into a definite shape of the exploratory machine as it was descending to the lowest of the ledges. She tried to see who was on board, but the bubble of the cockpit cover had been tinted so that it was like facing a blind thing which depended on other than human sense to attack.

As it touched down, the whir of the antigrav was stilled and the world about her lay in deep silence. There was no sound of bird or insect such as she might have expected from the growth spreading out from the foot of the staircase—and Zass had disappeared!

The bubble split in two and the first of the flitter passengers came out.

Thom! But who else? That had been no talent of the spaceman which had produced a creature perhaps a thousand years dead to drive once more into the open. He did not even look at her after one quick glance, but rather stood to one side as if he played only servant or guard to his companion.

The body that clambered out and put a scaled and webbed hand with thin fingers on Thom's shoulder in a gesture of comradeship was humanoid in shape but manifestly not as human as the young man with him, or even Simsa. The clothing it wore was far more abbreviated than Thom's— short breeches that came just a fraction down green-gray scaled thighs, a sleeveless shirt over which were numerous straps supporting a number of things which could be either tools or weapons. Around the head with the goggle eyes was a ruff of frilled flesh which stood erect, over which rippled flashes of vivid coloring as the alien stepped forward. A Zacathan!

This was one of the pacific nonwarriors of the galaxy, whose struggle was not against men or worlds, but rather to unravel and record the past—and whose long lives were dedicated to the belief that one scrap of knowledge added to their store was worth all the discoverer had to give.

But a Zacathan! She had not been aware that there had been one on board the spacer before her escape. Why had Thom not told her? Why had she not sensed such a brain when she had been able to pick up the dangerous musings of the officer and Greeta?

And what could they do? Build hallucinations—the wuul had been proof of that—and perhaps break such a memory block as she had put on Thom. What else?

She stared down the ledges, her eyes searching out those of the Zacathan and locking with them swiftly, so swiftly she had no time to deny it, mind to mind.

"What do you fear?" The evenly spaced words formed in her mind.

She answered with the truth before she could think clearly, his very presence had surprised her so. "You."

The saurian face was perhaps not constructed to easily form a smile, but she felt the gentle humor now in the other's mind touch.

"Am I then so formidable, gentle fem?"

"I think . . . yes—" Her eyes had narrowed. She had yet to marshal all that had come to her in this place, to truly make herself one with that other and those who had once stood behind her. "I think you are a very formidable person." She kept her voice low as she replied, not with mind touch (she wanted no more of that) but rather in the trade-lingo, aloud.

"As I think." Now he spoke and there was a hissing accent to his words. "It seems"—now his eyes released hers as he lifted his head a little to view the mass of ruin behind her—"that we have found something long sought."

"Chan-Moolan-plu." Out of the past she could no longer deny came that name, and immediately she knew what it stood for and why it was on this world.

"Chan-Moolan-plu," the Zacathan repeated. "Your home, gentle fem—once?"

She shook her head. "An outpost—a training place—before the Baalacki came." More and more the story awoke in her. No . . . home—home was— She shook her head again, not at any gesture or word from him, but because she knew that what she might say would mean nothing now. That planet which birthed the Elder One who was now a part of her was gone, vanished into a fog of time so great there was no reckoning it—in her own system of accounting years and seasons.

"And the Baalacki?" A little to her surprise, it was Thom who raised the question.

"They made this world as you see it. They"—she shrugged—"are long since gone. Each people who rise, look to the stars, and roam the outer reaches have enemies, or acquire them along the way. And then a day comes where there is a final battle-locking. One may go down to the dust, but it is also true that the victor is left wounded, perhaps to death, and another empire falls apart." She made a gesture as if shifting some of that sand still bubbling below between her fingers. "What are left . . ."

"What are left," the Zacathan broke in as she hesitated, "are shards and pieces scattered here and there—which we strive to bring together so that we may understand—"

"Why?" Simsa interrupted him in turn. "To learn this or that trick of knowledge which will give *you* power so that again the wheel will spin and you and your ships and your alliances of planets be reduced in turn?"

"Some seek for that, yes. Others for knowledge which has nothing to do with that sort of power, gentle fem. We are many races, many species—surely it was so then, was it not?"

"The Sorkel, the Vazax, the Omer—" In her mind she saw each she mentioned, scaled, winged, various-colored of flesh, different of brain patterns. "Yes, there were many of us and some who were always apart." Now she stared at the Zacathan in sudden enlightenment. "From whom, Lordly One, did you take your first memories?"

"Ah . . ." It was his turn to nod. "So you had your historians, also? As for our memories, those of my race are long and our archives go far back. We have our legends, also, gentle fem. That is why when I was informed of you I came with what swiftness this time and space afford. I was on Kaltorn when Thom"—she saw his fingers tighten on the young man's shoulder as if in affection—"sent a message by the mail launch. My dort-ship strove to match the flight pattern of the Star Climber, and your own actions pulled me thus to you."

Perhaps it was so, she could sense no evasion in his mind, whatever might be his speech. Yet different species . . . Yes, he could be weaving for her just such a pattern as she had purposefully set upon Thom. Upon Thom!

She spoke now to the spaceman. "You were never memory-changed!" Her words came out harshly, as if she accused him.

He shook his head and there was no curve to his mouth—that and his jaw were set grimly. "You succeeded," he told her in clipped words. "Only—"

"Only," the Zacathan broke in again, "there were certain signs of such tampering which are familiar to the initiated. It was not difficult to disperse the shadows once they were recognized."

She could have guessed that much. With all the knowledge that must be at his command, this burrower into the past could well have diagnosed what had happened to this follower and countered it.

Simsa raised the rod, pleased to see that there was a stronger beam at the tips of the two horns. "Then you know also that I am not one who can be caged so that which and what I am may be drained from me to increase another's power! Thom . . ." Simsa hesitated, studying his set face, his eyes which held no warmth—he might be carved from some of the stone of this denuded planet. "He"—she spoke not to the man whose whole attitude was a defense against her, but again to the Zacathan—"Thom was gone, apparently after he had delivered me into the hands of those who spied upon me, who strove to find ways to use what they thought I was. He was with one of those when I found him—they having traced me by some one of your machines upon which you depend so much. I had won free of what they had put or strove to put upon me. Why should he return to come ahunting again? If we wish to be simply truthful, I saved his life. He was going into the maw of one of those." She pointed the rod to the blob of the dead sand-thing, which still showed a little above the flood that had brought it here.

There was no change in Thom's expression, and she told herself she did not expect any understanding from him now. Their partnership had always been an uneasy one even when they had struggled into the lost city on Kuxortal, fighting shoulder to shoulder there against the outlaws who had laired within that spawn of vegetation-devoured buildings. She owed him— Perhaps she did owe him! Had he never led her into the forgotten ways, she would not have met with the Elder One—never have been more than a child playing at useless things—one without kin or friends. Yes, she owed him much for that! And now she made restitution in words:

"I owe you, Thom Chan-li." She used his formal name as one who lists debts. "There is no debt between us. I was wrong—the scales are even, or perhaps I owe you more for what I did in the valley. If so, demand your price of me now."

The Zacathan looked from the young man to Simsa and then back again, as one who stands aside and listens.

Thom raised a hand in a repudiating gesture. "You owe me nothing," he said coldly. And Simsa believed that had the Zacathan's hand not still imprisoned his shoulder, he would have turned back to the flitter and left her.

"Good!" It was the alien who put force into that, as if he were genuinely pleased that something had been resolved between them, even though it was manifest that nothing had been done at all. "Gentle fem, far from a cage—all honor and ease await you. Thom has told me that you had reason to mistrust certain ones on board the ship. Be sure that this was not our intention, nor could it have been carried out—not with Thom's message already on its way to me. And it seems"—now he glanced from her to the pile of the ruins— "that our suggestion that fate often moves on the behalf of believers is also right. For without your flitting from the ship and landing here, we would never perhaps have found this— what did you call it?—Chan-Moolan-plu, a place of your own people, once."

"A place of power." Something in him quieted all the uneasiness, even the stiffness of her mistrust. "A place of initiation."

"And you have passed that?"

He was very quick to catch her up, she thought. "Yes." Never would she enlarge upon that. What she had done by that poisonous pool was hers alone—not to be shared.

"I will warn you," she said swiftly, "that there are matters here best left alone. Thrusting too deep into ancient secrets can bring—death!"

His lizard jaws spread apart in what could only be thought a smile, showing formidable teeth. "There is always peril in the unknown," he returned. "If one listens to the whisperings of dangers to come, one remains in the shadow of danger without profit. Be sure we do not go recklessly upon any trace of that which we search for all our days. And—"

What more he would have added she would never know. For beneath her feet the ledge swayed. That hole from which the sand gushed was growing large. As on another world released floods of water could undermine bands and cliffs, so here the moving sand was carving itself a greater runway.

Out of the sky flashed Zass—the zorsal giving tongue as she flew straight for Simsa. The flitter lurched nearer to the sand flood and there was a rumbling from out of the ruins.

Without a word Thom sprang at her as she jumped in turn away from the forepart of the ruin. She had no time to defend herself against his grasp, to even move the rod, for he had her in a tight hold, the heating rod against her own body as he jerked her down the three ledges which were now tilting on the very brink of a raging flood, if one could so describe that wash of sand. And in it there moved more creatures, their sucker-grown and tentacled legs reaching out as they were borne along, some grasping the edge of the ledges for anchorage.

There came a crash that silenced even Zass's hoarse screams. Behind, some strained wall or floor had given way. But the Zacathan was waiting at the flitter and Thom bundled her forward into the hands of the lizard man. Those closed upon her in the same tight hold as Thom had used, and she was pulled into the outworld flyer, Zass streaking before her, Thom pushing at her from behind, so she sprawled backward into the luggage space behind the two seats at the fore of the bubble. Thom was in the pilot's seat and the bubble snapped down as he triggered a small lever on the board before him. The flitter arose so suddenly that Simsa, still unable to completely understand what had happened, flopped back again on the floor as the machine took to the air.

"Over it—on hold!" The Zacathan leaned far forward in the seat, his snouted nose pushed against the transparent covering of the cockpit. "No, not all of it—praise be to Zurl and Zack—a settling, but not all lost!"

Simsa edged up to a crouching position and endeavored to look below. She was in time to see the ledged stairway slip down to rise on the other side. And there had indeed been a toppling of some walls within.

"Cruise!" the Zacathan ordered again. "Let us see how bad it is."

Under Thom's control the flitter began to circle about the spread of the ruins. From this perch aloft, the girl could see how extensive the structure had been. For it was no town, she knew that. This had been something of a temple, something of a school—and even more a legend. The Elder One had never been here. Her initiation had taken place on another world. But she had heard of this doorway to even greater knowledge all her past life.

There sounded another roar above the noise of the flitter. Simsa shrank in upon herself as she watched a full quarter of the structure below her tremble and slide in. There was a new gushing on the side of the mound. Where the sand still poured and puddled there came a green flood to cut into that thick mixture, in a spate of energy that carried it on and over the sand toward the vegetation beyond.

Simsa was not aware of her own small cry until she heard it. The water of the initiation pool was flooding out—sinking into the sand, vanishing forever from ruin or day. There would never be another to come and submit to its testing, to open thus the realm beyond the world.

"Sooo—" The Zacathan's voice was close to a hiss, yet when she glanced at him there was nothing in his eyes but a shadow of loss and of pity.

She resented that pity for an instant and then she knew what lay behind it. Not that there was lost to him and his kind another discovery, perhaps one of the greatest they might ever make, but rather that she had lost something that was worth much to her.

"It is gone." She voiced the only thing she might say. "The life is gone."

And she spoke the truth. It seemed to her that now lay only the broken or rapidly breaking stone, that what she had sensed in the walls bled from the past glories, as the water of dreams bled from whatever buried channel contained or refreshed the pool. She was as sure as if she had walked again within or could see through that maze of walls, that the great hall was no more—that those thrones which had once served the leaders of her kind had toppled and gone the way that the years prevailed.

"No," the Zacathan said slowly in trader's speech, as if at this moment he had no wish to invade her tangled and sorrowing thoughts, "you live. What was once here only waited to serve the last of those who had laid its first stones upon stones. Let it be, Yan—"

Simsa was about to ask who Yan was when she realized the Zacathan had been speaking to Thom, using his friend name. He still did not acknowledge her presence and as the flitter wheeled outward and away from the ruin, she wondered if the choice the Zacathan had really made for her so forcibly back on the terraces was the right one.

As that exile of the valley had been before her—alone—so was she now. On Kuxortal she had had ties, tenuous as those had been. But old Ferwar had been a part of her life. There were those of her own generation in the Burrows who knew her, even though she had no close relationship with any of those outcasts. The Elder One had had her friends, companions, her clan-kin—now she had nothing except this thing that had happened to her by chance.

By chance? Zass chirruped in her ear and she reached up

her right hand to smooth the zorsal's small furred body. Was it chance that had brought the Life Boat to this forgotten world out of all the rest? She had always scoffed at the superstitions of the Burrowers and of those who followed the "gods" of the upper city—that anyone could be influenced by some unknown power about which they were largely ignorant was folly beyond folly.

Yet she had met with Thom merely by chance—had she been there at their meeting place a few breaths later, never would she have been drawn into the race across the haunted wilderness and therein met that which was the other part of her. And had she not picked up the thoughts concerning her on the spacer and taken off . . .

It was indeed folly to think that this was all part of some greater plan, that she had been moved by another will as a gaming piece might be shaken and moved! She was Simsa, she made *her* own choices—went her own way. But why had that way, seemingly by chance again, become her path to this place of the past wherein those of the Forerunners had achieved adeptship and the greater knowledge?

What had in turn given her the power to summon the river of sand and in the end bring about the destruction of that which had endured so long? The Zacathan— She hunched herself into a small space, both the rod and Zass clutched to her—all that remained truly her own was in that grasp. She could sense no guile in him. He had not wanted her power— only her knowledge. And the two of those were not one and the same but separate. She was warned and she was armed— not only by what the Elder One had done with her, but by the place of initiation. She had very much to learn—whereas when she had first met that other Simsa she had felt ready to conquer the world itself, now she was humble and a little afraid. Though that was within her, outwardly she must wear the mask of the Elder One's own imperturbable self.

The feathery softness of the zorsal's antennae brushed the ebony skin of her cheek, and Zass nipped lightly, caressingly, at the hand holding her small body. Zass . . . she was thankful for Zass and—

Once more she eyed the Zacathan measuringly. His head was turned a little away from her and he watched the last of the ruins slide by beneath them as they headed out over the barren rock that covered so much of this world. Yes, in him she could feel only some disappointment, a disappointment for the loss of that ancient seat of strange learning.

As if her very gaze upon him was like a touch on his shoulder or arm to summon his attention, his head swung around, the frill still erect and showing a faint shimmer of color over the scales there. He smiled.

"Not such a loss?" he asked strangely, as if he could read a thought that had not yet crossed her own mind. "A thing having served its purpose, can it not be discarded?"

Was that the truth? Had that invisible finger of fate pointed her straight to this place, in spite of all her belief in her own freedom, that she might be the last of her kind—

"Or the first, gentle fem?" Yes, he was reading her thoughts! For a moment she felt the heat of temper flash, and then she shrugged. She was without kin or country, or even world. If they found a place for her, why should she quarrel with that? She had never before put down roots—

"Why should you, if you wish it not?" the Zacathan continued. He read her thoughts but he spoke aloud, she was not certain why. "You are free to come or go, or stay—" He made a small gesture with his hand to indicate the country lying before them. "If that is your true wish?"

"No," she answered him also aloud this time. "I would . . ."

She hesitated. Would what? Go with these two and devote herself to their search for ancient knowledge? She studied the back of Thom's dark head. He was the first off-worlder she had ever met—and she had once thought that they were all alike. Now she knew that they were different, different as an upper city lord from a Burrow dweller. She had meddled—tried to fight him. Now, now she was glad that she had not been skillful enough to have accomplished her purpose. There was the officer and Greeta and there was Thom and this lizard man— Doubtless there were many other gradations of thought and feeling out among the stars and on other worlds. Who was she to sit in judgment over what she did not know?

"I would go with you" It seemed to her that she took long to make that decision, but perhaps it was only the space of a breath or two. Now she added, not using thought speech but the tongue of the spacemen and speaking directly to the back of Thom's head, "I would go with both of you."

"Well enough." That was the Zacathan. Thom had said nothing; he might be a mindless, uncaring part of the machine he guided. She waited.

It was important that he say some word, make some gesture. But he did not and she began to question the wisdom of her own choice. After all, what did he have to judge her by? He had his own people, he was no exile.

The flitter hummed on across the fissured bareness of the rock plain, but they were lifting higher into the haze. Now she could make out only patches of the rock as mist began to draw around them, cutting off the solid planet beneath. Zass moved uneasily in her grasp. She loosed her hold on the zorsal and the creature gave a small leap, first to land on the forearm of the Zacathan, then into Thom's lap.

The spaceman's hands were busied. Then he raised them from the board, but the flitter raced on. Apparently no controls were needed for a set course. His head turned a little, but she could only see one eye and a part of his cheek, and the corner of his mouth that had been set in so stern a band.

"No more tricks?" He asked that slowly, with a measured interval between each word.

She stiffened. Tricks? There had been no trickery between them ever. What she had always done was what had seemed right and just to her. Then the humor that underlay his question reached her.

There had been little of that emotion in the Burrows. She was awkward about responding to it, as strange in its way as some of the thoughts of the Elder One. But now it was also the Elder One within her who knew what he would do—he was purposely belittling what she had done, making it a thing of little account so that it could be dismissed, perhaps forgotten except as an object lesson for her to live with for a while (though she did not believe that he meant that, either!).

"No more tricks." She smiled, and the movements of her lips then felt strange and new, but this was good, this strangeness. "There is one . . ." She spoke, now, in a language she had not known until the words rose from some place deep within her. "There was one and another—and another—"

She left the rod lying across her bent knees and, leaning, she did something that Simsa of the Burrows would have shrunk from, what the Elder One would not perhaps have countenanced in her own time. What did it matter concerning those two? She was herself—still herself and what she chose to be. Her fingers touched with the lightness of Zass's antennae those two shoulders nearest herself—the scaled and the suit-covered one—just for an instant. But it was enough.

AUSTIN MEMORIAL LIBRARY
220 S. BONHAM
CLEVELAND, TEXAS 77327
713 592 3920